FIRE IN THE BARLEY

FIRE IN THE BARLEY

FRANK PARRISH
A DAN MALLETT NOVEL OF SUSPENSE

PERENNIAL LIBRARY
Harper & Row, Publishers
New York, Cambridge, Philadelphia, San Francisco
London, Mexico City, São Paulo, Sydney

First PERENNIAL LIBRARY edition published 1983.

Library of Congress Cataloging in Publication Data

Parrish, Frank.
    Fire in the barley.

    (Perennial library ; P/651)
    Reprint. Originally published: New York : Dodd,
Mead, 1977.
    I. Title.
PR6066.A713F5   1983   823'.914   82-48815
ISBN 0-06-080651-6 (pbk.)

83 84 85 86 10 9 8 7 6 5 4 3 2 1

FIRE IN THE BARLEY

I

Dan Mallett helped his mother to bed at half past ten. She needed help, increasingly, on the steep little stairs of the cottage. Every day she leaned more heavily on his arm or on her own two rubber-tipped sticks. Her face had once been as brown as his own – she was an active, outdoor body, in spite of certain grand ideas – but now it was white, as white and wrinkled as scrumpled tissue-paper. It grieved Dan to see her. Among all the lines on her face, lines of laughter and vexation, frown lines and puzzlement lines, there were lines of suffering.

It was her hips, and it was arthritis. Dr Smith in the village said so. There was no doubting it. But she wouldn't have an operation, wouldn't consider it, not on the National Health.

'Those big wards gi' me the jumps,' she said. 'All the people cheek b'jowl, the sweepin's o' the streets, nurses every colour you ever saw 'cep white, doctors comes an' prods you an' passes on wi' a sneer – '

'A sneer?' said Dan, startled at the picture of devilish, sneering doctors on their rounds in the County Hospital.

She would have it that they sneered, sneered and sniffed. She had seen them at it when his father died. Nothing would induce her to go near them. They pained her more and more, those hip joints, but nothing would induce her into the contemptuous, aseptic inhumanity of the free hospital.

Something would have to be done about it, but Dan didn't yet see his way.

He would have heated her some water on the range, but the night was warm and she said she'd do very well with cold water.

5

He kissed her cheek.

He said, 'I'm sorry, old lady,' thinking confusedly of the pain of her hips, the steep little stairs of the cottage, her disappointment in him.

'It's like your dad,' she said. 'I'd sooner have him as he was than not have him.'

Dan nodded and closed her door softly.

He went downstairs and took a four-hour nap, setting the alarm in his head to wake him at 3 in the morning. It did; he crept upstairs to his own bedroom to change. He put on dark trousers, rubber-soled boots which laced up tight over his ankles, and a coat of drab browny-green tweed. The whole of the lower part of the lining of the coat was double, with large slits in each skirt, to form a single capacious pocket. Dan had given the pocket a removable lining of American cloth, which could be taken out and sponged clean of the blood of pheasants, partridges, woodcock, hares, trout and other cargoes.

Downstairs, Dan pocketed a pencil flashlight and a clasp-knife. He filled a battered silver hunting-flask from the bottle of whisky in the kitchen cupboard. He put on his cap, and picked up a home-made blackthorn stick with a heavy lump of metal in the knob.

He switched off the lights, went out, locked the door, and tucked the key in a gap between bricks behind a drainpipe.

The dogs started whining affectionately at him; the terrier yapped. He quieted them: 'Hush, Pansy. Hush, Nimrod. Quiet there, silly bitch, silly Goldie.'

The dogs woke the bantams, who began clucking with sleepy bad temper in their coops. Some of the pigeons scraped and thumped in their loft, and a squab began its peremptory whining for food.

Ignoring the roads completely – he seldom used them at night – Dan set off for the river woods beyond Yewstop. He crossed the ground fast, without seeming to hurry. It was very warm, even at 3.15 in the morning, a breathless night in late July. There were clouds in the sky, but between them stars; after a few

6

minutes Dan could see quite well enough to avoid falling down a hole or catching on wire or making any noise.

After ten minutes he was on Fred Mortimer's land. After twenty-five minutes he was still on it. It was a very big property now, and very well farmed. Dan skirted a twenty-acre wheat-field, ripening towards harvest; from what he could see in the starlight, it looked a beautiful crop. Fred certainly knew how to farm, and he knew a lot of other things too. Dan had plenty of respect for him, and Dan was not given to respecting people.

Dan reached the corner of the wheat-field, slid under the hedge, and started across a ten-acre pasture.

He was surprised to see a car going slowly along the lane a quarter of a mile away. It was a back lane, little used, passing only Yewstop Farm where Willie Martin lived, and then joining the Milchester road. The car went straight past the farm gates, so it was nothing to do with Willie Martin. It was crawling along at a walking pace. If it was going to Milchester, where was it going from? The lane had never been used, in Dan's memory, at this hour of the night.

The car stopped and its lights went out. The driver needed a slash? He had a girl with him? He was sleepy?

Dan paused, mildly curious, watching and listening. He did not want to be seen or heard himself. He did not hear the door of the car, or any sort of movement. Then he heard voices. His hearing was good and the night was absolutely still; he could hear two men's voices, but not whose voices they were or what they were saying. Still no car door had opened. It might be two men sitting in the car and talking, but Dan was sure one voice belonged to a man who was standing in the lane. Dan thought that man had come quietly along the road to where the car was, or else had been waiting for it. Why wait so long before talking? To make sure the car was alone? The driver was alone?

It wasn't a chance meeting. It couldn't be, at that time and place. The car had gone there to meet the man. The man had

7

gone there to meet the car. Yewstop Lane was a place they could meet without anybody seeing them.

The car's lights came on and the engine started. It drove away slowly; the lights disappeared round the corner of the river woods.

Dan thought it very odd. In the ten years since he had left the bank and the town, and pulled off his dark blue suit and his little pointed black shoes, he had been out and about at 4 in the morning perhaps a thousand times. He had seen many peculiar things. But he had never seen a furtive meeting, obviously planned, between a car and a pedestrian, in a back lane. Nobody had got into the car, because no door had opened and closed. Therefore the pedestrian was still in the lane. Why was he? What could anybody be doing there? Why choose such a place and time for a conversation? Was this second man in Dan's line of business, bound for the river woods? Was the man in the car his mate? His employer? That seemed terribly unlikely. Were they burglars? Was the car carrying away something the other man had stolen? Stolen from Willie Martin at Yewstop Farm? But Willie had nothing worth stealing.

Dan was curious. He was also extremely anxious not to have his own plans mucked up by outsiders. On both counts he wanted to see who this was, hanging about in Yewstop Lane at 4 in the morning, and what he was carrying, and what he was doing.

Like a shadow, like a fox, Dan crossed the pasture towards the lane where the car had stopped. His rubber-soled boots made no sound on the grass, which had been eaten to the closeness of a lawn by Fred Mortimer's dairy cows. He thought he'd hear movement; he might see the man in the starlight, although the lane was hedged and sunken. He was still fifty yards from the lane when he heard a faint shuffling and rustling noise, a muffled clang of boot-sole on metal, and then a metallic tick-tick-tick.

It was a bicycle. The man was away. He was off down the lane towards the river.

Dan shrugged. It was all very intriguing, but he had other things to think about. He went on to the lane and across it, where the car had stopped, having to push his way through big bullfinch hedges on both sides. He went on to Willie Martin's land. He gave a wide berth to Yewstop Farm, as Willie had a noisy collie in a kennel. He went on towards the river woods. The woods belonged to Willie but he let the shooting. They were boggy, and there was a big stretch of marshy waste beyond, where the river divided. For these reasons it was a great place for woodcock, the only good woodcock shooting for miles round. Quite a lot of birds bred there. Most of them went away in the winter, but Dan was sure a few stayed. Many more came from abroad, a little smaller and paler than the local birds, to feed on the marsh in hard weather.

The birds lay hidden in the undergrowth all day, even after they'd hatched their chicks. They were even better camouflaged than partridges, a sort of marbling of buff and reddish brown and black, sometimes completely invisible, even from a few feet away, when they squatted still as death among twigs and dead leaves. Several times, with or without a dog, Dan had disturbed a hen-bird crouched on her chicks in the nest. When this happened, the mother carried the chicks away, out of danger, in the most extraordinary way. Sometimes she held them between her feet, sometimes between her legs, and sometimes pressed against her chest by her long straight bill. Dan imagined the old birds carried the chicks in the same various ways when they went out to the marsh to feed; but he had never seen them do so, as they only fed in pitch darkness.

Dan had often wondered how they found worms under the mud at night. They poked about with their long sharp bills, and stood with their heads on one side as though they were listening. Dan's father had always said they *were* listening, but Dan found it hard to believe that even a woodcock could hear the movements of a worm under the mud. He was more inclined to believe his father's other theory, that they stamped their feet to imitate rain and bring the worms to the surface.

They were wonderful, fascinating, mysterious birds, unlike any others. They even had their ears in a different place, in front of and below their big brown eyes.

Before dawn they went back into the woods, weaving silently down the rides to their hiding-places. They kept the same hours as foxes. These resident birds bred early, much earlier than most birds. They were sitting on their mottled eggs before the end of March. So by now, by the end of July, there should be plenty of plump young birds. They wouldn't be shot for a long while. It was time for the drawnet. Dan's mother liked roast woodcock as well as anything.

It was very dark in the woods. Here and there the ground squelched underfoot. There was a smell of mud, wet leaf-mould, rotten wood. Toadstools grew in great noxious clumps, and shelves of hard brown fungi encrusted the fallen willow trees. As Dan went into the wood a particular smell, a horrible smell, struck his nostrils. He knew it was a stinkhorn toadstool; by day he would have seen a sort of squat phallus, with a shiny black head and a white stalk.

Dan went without hesitation down one of the big rides, which Willie Martin kept clear for his shooting tenants. He knew it was a normal route for the returning woodcock to take: they liked a familiar road and they liked plenty of room. Dan was looking for a particular big fir tree with a fallen willow behind it. The fir tree had a branch sticking out over the ride. An oak tree opposite also had an overhanging branch. The two branches would carry Dan's net.

He found the fir tree and pushed softly into the undergrowth. He crouched beside the roots of the willow. He switched on his pocket flashlight and put it in his mouth. He swept a covering of earth and dead leaves off a rough grid of sticks, and groped into a hole in the roots. He pulled out a plastic sack, one of the indestructible blue ones the farmers bought fertilizer in. It was tied tightly at the neck. Dan carried the sack into the ride and cut the string. He drew out the net and the other equipment. It was much easier, he found, to have your kit on the spot, instead of lugging it to and fro. If anyone should happen to find it, it didn't have his name on it.

The net was green nylon with a half-inch mesh, intended for soft fruit. The method was ancient, simple, and effective. The net hung between the overhanging branches, all four corners secured. When a cock flew into it, pulleys enabled Dan to let it down with a run, enveloping the bird. That, in essence, was all there was to it.

Dan uncoiled a length of thin, strong nylon cord which had a heavy iron nut tied to one end. He tossed the nut over the jutting branch of the fir tree. The other end of the cord was looped to a pulley. More cord ran through the pulley. Dan drew the pulley up so that it hung just below the branch, and tied the free end of the cord to the trunk of the fir tree. He hung another pulley from the oak branch on the other side of the ride. The cords from the pulleys he tied to the upper corners of his net. By walking backwards, he drew the net up so that it hung right across the ride. He could not see it, but he knew it was there: the top of the net was snubbed up against the pulleys. He tied down the lower corners of the net to the two trees.

The net was not very high. It didn't have to be. Woodcock kept low, flying through a wood in the dark.

Holding the cords, Dan hid himself and his clobber beside the ride. The woodcock would come back from their dinner on the marsh, flying low, slow, keeping to the ride, as though unsure of the way, as though frightened of bumping into trees in the dark. They'd be completely silent – they hardly ever made any noise except when they were courting. When a bird flew into the invisible net, Dan would let the net down with a rush and imprison it. Like his pheasant snares and his partridge-net, it was much more merciful than a bad shot. He would get the net up again quick, with the pulleys, ready for another woodcock. With luck he'd have a brace or two before first light.

He waited, infinitely patient, motionless; even by daylight

he would have been almost as invisible as the crouching cock himself. He passed the time in wondering who had been in Yewstop Lane, at 4 o'clock in the morning.

He sensed rather than saw the first fat woodcock come weaving uncertainly up the ride, stumpy and awkward, long bill pointed at the ground, flying almost like an owl. It plunged itself into the nylon strawberry net. Dan let go of his cords. The net collapsed on the ground, enveloping the bird, which began to flap and bump in panic. Dan ran forward. He didn't want the net torn; he did want it up again as soon as possible. He killed the bird, being careful not to damage the head, the brain being the great delicacy. He did it in the dark, making almost no noise, so as not to alarm the next birds. He began to extricate the bird's feet from the net in which they were entangled.

At that moment he heard the bloodhounds.

He was completely puzzled. Bloodhounds at this time of night could only mean police. Other people hunted with them for fun, but not at this time of night and not at this time of year. Who were the police after?

Of course, they were after the man in the lane, the man who had met the car, talked to the driver, and then gone off on his bicycle. Those two were doing something the police knew about. Well, they were burglars. Or they were spies, one spy with a bicycle handing military secrets to another spy with a car.

The bloodhounds were getting nearer. Dan thought: they're not after me. Then he thought: but they are.

The police had kept away from the place, so as not to alert the villains: but they had been ready. They'd brought the bloodhounds to the meeting-place, knowing exactly where to come and when. That was no good to them, because the bicyclist hadn't left a line of scent, not unless he rode along brushing his side against a hedge. But Dan had. Going through those thick mixed bullfinches he'd brushed against hundreds of leaves, and left a scent on every one. No hound could miss it. They might have hunted heel, following his line backwards across Fred Mortimer's land and all the way home to the cottage. But they hadn't. They'd hunted him the right way, and they were still hunting him. There'd be a screaming scent on the damp floor of the wood.

One good thing – the only good thing – was that the bloodhounds would be held to the pace of their handlers. They might slip them, but in the darkness Dan doubted it. But the sky would begin to lighten soon. That made things very different. The policemen would use their eyes, though the bloodhounds wouldn't. It was no good hiding from the sight of the men somewhere where the hounds could scent him; it was no good going where the hounds couldn't follow if the men could see him. He couldn't afford to be caught, not with his reputation. If he went to gaol, what would happen to his mother? An institution? It would drive her mad and then kill her.

The drawnet, pulleys and cords would have to be abandoned. It was useless trying to hide them hereabouts – the dogs would find them. It was too risky to carry. The woodcock likewise. Dan tossed it as far as he could into the undergrowth, which was a terrible shame.

The cry of the bloodhounds was nearer.

Dan ran away from the hounds, on down the ride. Short of flying, there was no possible way he could foil his line to baffle the hounds, not these hounds. He could run in circles like a hare, double back, cross and recross his line, retrace his own steps, climb trees, wade along streams: the bloodhounds would still follow. They could own his line on the surface of water, across a railway or on any road.

There was one way of stopping them. Maybe. Everything depended.

2

Dan hurried along the broad ride. He made much better speed, and went quieter, than if he took to the undergrowth: but the bloodhounds would go just as fast in the undergrowth. He looked in the dark for a small cross-ride, found it, and ran down it to the left. He turned left again after fifty yards down another main ride. He was going back towards the hunt, but fifty yards east of it. The bloodhounds wouldn't skirt or cut corners; they'd follow the exact line he'd taken. He could hear the dogs now, excited, certain, the scent breast-high and fresh. He could hear the policemen, too. They weren't making a lot of noise, but enough to stop Dan having to worry about any slight noise he might make.

Dan neared the eastern edge of the wood. He slowed down and went very cautiously, keeping to the edge of the ride. He expected them to have posted a man at the mouth of this other ride: and they had. He saw a gleam of starlight on a silver button. No starlight reached Dan under the thick green roof of the wood.

Dan crept to within fifteen yards of the edge of the wood. At one side of it, leaning against a tree, Dan could make out the shape of the policeman. He was not smoking, for a wonder. Dan was nearly sure he was alone: two would have been talking. People did, in the dark: it kept away evil spirits, and stopped the eye seeing monsters.

Dan softly withdrew twenty yards up the ride. He had very little time for his next trick. He went down on his knees at the edge of the ride. He crawled along, groping into the undergrowth, his fingers searching. After a horribly long time he found what he was looking for – two heavy chunks of rotten wood, bits of a fallen oak branch.

The bloodhounds had stopped. They were wildly excited. They had found Dan's scent spread all over the place, over the ride and each side of it; they had got to the drawnet. Torches would be switched on and the drawnet examined. The policemen might not know what it was. Very few people knew the old-time ways of catching birds. The police would hurry on down the ride, but they'd leave a man to guard the place until it could be searched by daylight.

Dan threw one of the chunks of wet, heavy wood as far as he could into the undergrowth. It made a lot of noise, landing in a mass of scrubby stuff. The policeman at the mouth of the ride couldn't fail to hear it. He'd wonder what to do. He'd probably stay put.

Dan made a noise like an excited bloodhound; he whimpered and gave tongue, softly, at the side of the ride.

The policeman would wonder what the hell another dog was doing by itself in the middle of the wood. He'd still stay put.

Dan shouted, in a shrill voice quite unlike his own, 'Hey, get off me! Get this dog off me! I surrender!'

Dan threw the other chunk of wood into the undergrowth. He made more bloodhound noises. Then he slipped across the ride and crouched behind a clump of hazel.

The policemen clumped up the ride, a huge flashlight glaring in front of him. He was shouting. He crashed into the undergrowth, waving his flashlight round.

Dan emerged from the hazels, sped down the ride and ran out of the wood.

He'd solved a minor problem but not the major one. Real bloodhounds were still behind him, and not far behind.

He trotted uphill across a field of roots. It was dry, crumbly soil, very unlike the boggy floor of the river woods, but the bloodhounds would know where he had gone. He got on to Willie Martin's back farm-track, brick-hard and deep-rutted.

The first beginnings of dawn were showing in the east. Dan's time was running out. He trotted down the track towards the farm.

The farm was completely dark. The collie scented or heard Dan, and began to bark with hysterical fury. Nothing could be done about that.

Dan turned when he got to the farmyard, and ran along the back of the big barn. He came to a fence of metal tubing, and climbed over it on to the concrete apron outside the milking-shed.

How tidy was Willie Martin after his evening milking? Had they scraped up the muck, sluiced the concrete from a hydrant? A heavy, comforting odour of cowdung hung like a fog over the yard. Dan's boots squelched. He sighed with relief. The concrete was a sea of fresh, wet muck, with a wholesome, powerful, pungent smell. Dan shuffled about in the muck, as the cows waiting to be milked had done. He was careful to slither everywhere, so as to leave no clear print of his rubber boot-soles.

The eastern sky was paler. The collie was barking like a maniac. In the pauses between its barks, Dan heard from the direction of the woods the baying of the police bloodhounds.

Dan went into the big barn between the milking-shed and the farmhouse. In a corner, where he expected, he found a pile of sacks of chemical fertilizer. The stuff stained a scent quite as badly as farmyard muck. Dan slit one of the plastic sacks, near the bottom, with his knife. The cut would look like a split, Dan thought. Powder gushed out on to the floor of the barn; he could not see it, but he knew it to be coarse and whitish. Dan picked up handfuls of it and strewed it about. It would hardly be visible on the dirty concrete floor; the bloodhounds would hate it.

He shone his pencil flash, for a second, at the slit bag of chemical. His idea was to scatter it behind him when he left the farm. The muck and the fertilizer, between them, would kill his scent for the bloodhounds. But the police would lead the bloodhounds in a big circle round the farm, like huntsmen doing a 'round-your-hat' cast with foxhounds after a check. The dogs would pick up the line of Dan's scent again, and follow him all the way home. The delay would give him time, but not enough, so a powdering of chemical fertilizer behind him was a good idea. But he couldn't carry one of the full sacks if he wanted to hurry. And it would be difficult to distribute the stuff in the right quantity. If he put down too little, the bloodhounds' marvellous noses would penetrate the smell and find his scent. If he put down too much, he'd make a visible white trail, like a paper-chase, for the policemen's eyes. He wondered, with a bit of anxiety, how to carry enough of the stuff with him, and how to scatter it behind him as he went. Then he had a stroke of luck. The beam of his flash flickered on a pair of gumboots – big, newish, green rubber, very mucky. Whatever they smelled of, it wouldn't be Dan. He pulled off his own boots and pulled on the gumboots. They were far too big for him, but he could get along in them.

Holding his own boots, he hurried out of the barn. The dog was still barking. Lights had been switched on in the farmhouse. The Martins were disturbed by the dog, naturally, that being what a watchdog was for. They'd come out and see what it was barking at.

Dan got away from the farmhouse as quickly as possible, from the collie and Willie's shotgun and the police bloodhounds. He had to move in a ridiculous shuffling gait, or the gumboots would have fallen off. He shuffled as fast as he could along Willie's farm-road towards the lane. He was careful to touch nothing, to let not so much as a head of cow-parsley brush against his hand or his trousers. It didn't do to underestimate bloodhounds. In time, in some mysterious way, Dan's own scent would drift down on to the outside of the boots, or penetrate the rubber outwards from his feet. Then the scent he left would be his. But for a while the scent he was leaving was Willie Martin's cows, the chemical fertilizer, and Willie himself.

The sky was getting paler rapidly. The collie had quietened

down. A few birds were singing. It was not the full chorus of early summer – just a greenfinch making a gentle gargle (prettier than its proper song, which was like a comb dragged along a hacksaw), a yellow-hammer asking for a bit of bread with no cheese, and a wren making a commotion in the bullfinch hedge by the lane. Over their clamour, Dan heard the bloodhounds come out of the river woods and race across the rootfield towards the farm. They'd been slipped, or the handlers were running like roe-deer. Good luck to them.

Dan came out on to the lane. He looked up and down it carefully. There must be a police car near, probably at least two. But there was nothing to be seen or heard. He shuffled along the lane as fast he he could, looking for a place where he could climb out without touching anything. He found a gap in the bullfinch filled by two strands of barbed wire. He climbed up the bank and through the wire and headed towards home.

He was back on Fred Mortimer's land. It was a part of the farm he seldom crossed, because it was not on his way to anywhere. It was not on anybody's way to anywhere. This was ground Fred had only bought a year before, paying £800 an acre to old Walter Newton's executors. Walter had let it run down badly; he had simply got tired, in his old age – he couldn't be bothered. Dan looked about him, with mild interest. Fred would soon put the land right.

After five minutes Dan came to a place he hadn't looked at for a long time, certainly not since Fred had bought it. In the faint, pearly light he saw that he was skirting a field of barley. On two sides, where there were trees and a hedge, Fred had left broad headlands. The crop was dirty, It was full of self-seeded oats, wild oats, couch-grass and poppies. Fred hadn't had time to clean the ground. Dan was surprised Fred hadn't put it down to turnips or potatoes, until he got it fit for cereals.

Well, Fred knew more about farming than Dan did. He knew so much about it that the other farmers copied him. Maybe some of the others would sow barley in dirty fallows, reckoning that if it was good enough for Fred it was good enough for them.

They all trusted Fred. Everybody liked him, too, in spite of his success. He had inherited 300 acres and now farmed 1,500. At one time he'd owned a share of the betting-shop in Milchester; maybe he still did; maybe that was where he'd got the capital to expand. Now he drove a Bentley, hunted in a black coat, and sent his sons to boarding school; and his daughter was married to an officer in the army. She was a powerful snob, from what Dan heard. Now where had he heard an ill-natured thing like that?

He remembered the tone of the voice saying it – 'Ooh, she's a powerful snob.' A girl's voice, not very refined. The voice gave him the face, and the face gave him the name. Janice. Fred's secretary. He had a full-time secretary, which was rare even on a farm as big as Fred's. Janice was a pretty girl, a little dark one with a neat figure. Dan had had his eye on her, but before anything came of it she had left the place. There was talk about that, but in a small village there was always talk.

The long walk home across the fields was soothing. It was a beautiful morning, and the world was full of living things. Dan watched nature not as a naturalist, a 'nature lover', like parsons or colonels' wives or schoolteachers on holiday, but as a fellow-inhabitant of woods and hedgerows and open spaces. He preyed on some of his small wild neighbours, as they preyed on each other.

The cornfields were changing colour almost as you watched. The pink bindweed rioted at their edges, sometimes climbing right up the stalks of the crop. At this time of day the little pink flowers were just opening in the growing warmth of the air; by night they'd be dead. Yellow ragwort and blue thistles made bright splashes of colour on grazing-land, bad grazing-land. Animals wouldn't eat either. They wasted an awful lot of pasture, but spraying them out took money, more money than most farmers had these days. Some of the apples were changing colour, the early varieties like Worcesters. The russets and Coxes and big cookers would be green for a while yet. The yaffles were banging and laughing in the big trees, after weeks of silence. Foreigners shot them, Dan had heard, but he couldn't think why; he wouldn't fancy eating a woodpecker. The titmice, finished with their breeding, were forming big groups and bustling about the countryside. The long-tailed titmice, piping softly to each other, hurried through the upper branches of the hedgerow trees. They had no special meaning for Dan, but he noted them instinctively, as he noted everything he saw.

Knowing what he was looking for, and knowing where to look, Dan took a slight detour; he found a late-sitting partridge. She had nine eggs on the ground, under a hedge at the edge of a six-acre fallow. The nest was a hollow, well hidden by the hedge, untidily lined with grass and leaves. The eggs were a pale olive colour, slightly pointed. When the hen-bird left the nest she would cover them over with dead leaves to hide them. She and Dan had many of the same ideas, including camouflage. Hers was excellent – a mass of brownish and blackish and reddish squiggles on a grey background. Dan wondered why this hen was so late with her eggs. He was sure partridges only had one brood. He guessed she'd been disturbed on earlier tries, by silage-making, hay-making, maybe a boy or a dog. The cheepers would be far too young to fly when partridge shooting started. Dan wondered whether to take some of the eggs and put them under a broody bantam-hen. He decided against it. But he might come back with a fine nylon net for the chicks. He'd handle them tenderly, put them in a rabbit-run, and fatten them up on corn and beans.

It got lighter by the second. Dan went carefully, although there was nobody about as early as this.

Then, in the distance, he saw a car: a white car, with something on top: a police car. It was on the main road from Milchester, heading towards the village. It still had its lights on, but it didn't need them. The sky was absolutely clear. The only mist was a curling ribbon which lay along the surface of the river. The police car was in a hurry, roaring towards the village. Dan wondered what was up. He was sure it was something to do with the bloodhounds. He'd be in the village later in the morning; he thought he'd hear something.

Meanwhile he was in a hurry too. He took off the big green gumboots and stuck them down the mouth of a drain. He was sorry to deprive Willie Martin, but he did not let it prey on his mind. He made better time in his own boots, and got home just at sunrise.

The dogs greeted him with quiet passion. He leaned into the kennel to pull their ears. His father had only had the one old lurcher, but Dan had bigger ideas. He had a lurcher himself, almost pure greyhound with a slightly broken coat, a pointer, and a half-bred Jack Russell terrier. They were all working dogs, highly trained specialists. They needed the very best food, and they got it. When they needed a vet's attention, they got the very best of that, too. They did so much for Dan that he thought it only right to look after them as well as he could. They were all worth a lot of money, but no money would have bought any of them

Dan went in. His mother was wide awake and fretful. He took her up a cup of tea, strong and sweet and milky. He told her his night had been a washout.

'Serve you right,' she said, sitting up in bed and sipping her tea. There were lines of suffering and sleeplessness on her face. The pain of her arthritis kept her awake, although she never admitted it.

Dan cooked breakfast, then fed his bantams and pigeons. It was now the hour when respectable men kissed their wives, hurried out to their cars, and rushed through dense crowds into their daily prisons. Dan sighed contentedly as he thought of them all, and had an hour's sweet sleep on his bed.

Old Mrs Mallett hobbled into his room as he slept. She looked down at him. Her disappointment, as always, sat on her head like a sandbag. She was a hen with one chick. She had hoped too much for him, wished too hard for him to rise in the world, sit in a respectable office, wear a neat white collar and a neat dark suit. It could so easily have happened. It *had* happened, until he had betrayed her. He had the brains and the energy; he even had the education. He could have been Assistant Manager of the bank in Milchester by now. And what was he? An odd-job man, a poacher, a bad character, no better than his father.

Old Mrs Mallett sighed, picturing the might-have-been. Her mind's eye saw a neat new house in a private road at the edge of Milchester. Her ewe lamb driving home in a neat little car, hurrying up the path between shaven lawns with his briefcase in his hand, wiping shiny black shoes on the doormat, sitting down for an hour before supper to look at urgent papers. 'They've asked me to be Manager of a new branch . . . I must put in a call to New York . . . They want me to stand for the County Council . . . Yes, I owe all my success to my mother . . .'

The rosy picture faded, abashed by brutal reality. Instead of the gracious little house of her dreams, here they still were in the crazy old gamekeeper's cottage in the shadow of the dripping woods. Instead of being at the edge of the town, handy for buses and shops, here they still were in the depths of the boggy wilderness. Instead of a shiny new car, the boy came home on his ancient bicycle, more often at 6 in the morning than 6 in the evening. Instead of a briefcase he was apt to be carrying a brace of pheasants or a fat trout.

He'd been asleep most of the previous afternoon, when respectable men were dictating letters in glossy offices. That was because he was out in the small hours, when respectable men were snoring in chintzy bedrooms. And he'd been a scholarship boy at the Grammar School! And he'd been a trainee at the bank! And they might by now be calling him 'Mr Mallett', and bringing him papers to sign . . .

As though he felt her eyes on him, her son opened his own eyes and grinned. Mrs Mallett smiled back. It was not what she meant to do. She couldn't help herself. She'd been bewitched by that grin all her life, since she was eighteen, first

22

on the father's face and now on the son's. So the respectable, ambitious greengrocer's daughter married the gamekeeper-turned-poacher; so the respectable, ambitious widow kept house for the banker-turned-poacher. Like father like son, too like, all too like. The father was here in the son's flesh, as well as in his wicked ways. It was the same small, spare, wiry body, much stronger than it looked, that could wriggle like an eel, and creep like a spider, and lie as still as a stone. The same small, wedge-shaped face, deeply weatherbeaten, that looked as though butter wouldn't melt in its mouth. The same untidy brown hair, with the tuft that stuck out at the back. And the same bright blue eyes, innocent as a young girl's, cherub's eyes, disarming as a kitten, misleading as a cat.

A lad for the girls, the father had been. They couldn't say no to him. She was one of the ones that couldn't. Like father like son. Mrs Mallett heard nothing about that side of her son's life – he didn't kiss and tell – but she didn't need it spelled out for her. They'd want to mother him, coddle him, take him on their laps, feed him up. Much he needed any of that, but he'd smiled his wide, sweet, innocent smile, and take whatever was offered, and plenty that wasn't . .

Dan Mallett looked up at his mother, knowing quite well what she was thinking. He was sad to have disappointed her, but you couldn't turn a foxcub into a fantail just by wishing.

He'd tried, driven by her, by her pride and ambition and hope. He'd sat the scholarship and gone to the Grammar School, and worn a blazer with a shield on the pocket, and made friends with the sons of land-agents and building-contractors, and with a parson's son, a doctor's, an army officer's. She'd encouraged these friendships, drowning his father's doubts, pushing him off to play tennis and meet nice families. He began to speak like a gentleman, and act like a gentleman, and think like a gentleman. And she kept him at his homework in the evening, and packed him off to bed at a sensible hour, and he dreamed . . .

Of being out in the woods with his father, at 4 in the morning, laying the artful horsehair loops across the creepways of the pheasants.

Armed with good reports and good examination results, Dan had gone to the bank in his new blue suit. They took him on. He was a Management Trainee. No future was beyond him. His mother was speechless with joy. His father was awed, impressed in spite of himself. Dan himself felt a mixture of triumph and dismay. He was proud to have justified his mother's faith, repaid her sacrifice and penny-pinching. But he felt like a half-grown pheasant with its neck in one of those horsehair loops.

All went well. He worked hard. He was natty in dress, smooth in manner, adroit with figures, good with customers. He was sent off on courses, and came back with new skills and new contacts. He had lodgings in Milchester. He took a colleague's sister out to dinner, and ate scampi by candlelight. The broad highroad lay straight before him.

Then his father had to hide, most of one night, in a wet ditch, while the keepers beat the hedgerows round him. He was ill next day and dead next week. His legacy was a twelve-bore gun, a bundle of nets, a lurcher dog and a bad reputation. Dan decided to take them all on.

His father's death did not change him. It simply brought him face to face with something he had known for years. He hated the bank. He loathed the town. He detested the broad straight highroad stretching drearily before him. His one idea was to dive off the road into the hedges and ditches. He peeled off his prison uniform, his sober banker's suit. He tore the shackles from his neck, his demure collar and tie. He struck off his urban ball and chain, and fled back into the woods where he belonged. It was a terrible blow to his mother, but he saved his own soul and his sanity.

He avoided having to marry his colleague's sister. He avoided a lifetime of deep-frozen scampi, supermarket Riesling, and arrangements of dead flowers in brass vases.

Dan was booked that morning to cut Sir George Simpson's grass: the croquet lawn with the Suffolk Punch, the orchard with the Hayter, the rough at the bottom with the Allen Scythe. He did not at all dislike strolling along behind these efficient, self-propelled machines.

His mother violently disliked his doing such menial jobs. It was not what he had gone to the Grammar School for, not what the bank had trained him for. She would have disliked it even more if she'd ever seen him at it, putting on an act as a home-spun peasant, speaking as broad as her own grandfather. But the act amused Dan, and it was worth several pounds a week to him.

He bicycled to the village, stopping on the bridge to look at the river. It was absolutely smooth in the windless morning, 200 yards of flawless mirror from the bridge to the bend. The weed had been cut, but bars had been left, the width of the river, as larders and shelter for the fish. A family of moorhens with half-grown young was puddling by the sedge which fringed the bank. A grey wagtail strutted along a boom in the water, put there to catch the weed when it was cut. There were no swallows or swifts over the water, because at this time of day no fly was hatching out of it. Thirty yards upstream there was plop, and a ring appeared in the glassy water, widening as it came down-stream. It might have been a trout rising to a hatching dun, but Dan was certain, for reasons he could not have defined, that it was a dabchick. Sure enough, as he watched, the little reddish head appeared near the bank. The dabchick had swum under the water, almost as fast as a fish. They looked extraordinary when they did that, like rats. Dan was rather fond of them, but he saw how they irritated fishermen.

Dan looked straight down into the clear water, where the current had gouged a deep place under the bridge. He had some-times seen very big trout here, three and four pounders, keeping in the shade, never coming near the surface, probably cannibals.

But all he saw today was a school of small grayling weaving about in the depths.

A hundred yards upstream, Dr Smith's lawn sloped to the water; Dan mowed that one, too, when the Doctor's sons were away. Beyond the lawn were a shrubbery and a kitchen garden, divided from the river-bank by six yards of rough-mown grass. Dan worked in the kitchen garden sometimes; it had been keeping his mother in asparagus in May, strawberries in June, raspberries in July. Dan could grow little in his own garden, which was overhung by dripping trees.

Beyond the kitchen garden were the extensive stewponds, which the Doctor had dug a dozen years before; they were fed by a runnel from the main river. The Doctor was an expert and passionate dry-fly fisherman. He had started the syndicate which leased nearly all the fishing for four miles above the village, as far as Willie Martin's woods. They bought fingerling rainbows from a hatchery, and fattened them in the stews. They put most in at a pound and a quarter, but they kept a few to go in much bigger than that. They were lovely trout. They soon turned as shy as a wild brown trout in the river – just as fussy, just as difficult to catch – but they were tame in the stews. You could get all you wanted in two minutes with a handful of pellets and a landing-net. Dan's mother liked a fresh grilled trout for her supper.

Something burst away from the bank by the stewponds. It was a coot, almost black except for the white front of its face; it ran across the surface of the water, splashing madly with its big awkward feet. It might have been trying to fly; if so, it changed its mind and settled back on to the water, bobbing its head like an old schoolteacher getting the right answer. Something had alarmed the bird. Somebody was at the stewponds. No doubt young Harry Barnett, the syndicate's water-keeper.

Dan crossed the bridge, looked right, and saw the police car outside the Doctor's house. He should now have turned left, past the Post Office, to get to Sir George's; but curiosity sent him pedalling along to the Doctor's. It occurred to him also that he wanted to talk to the Doctor. He went slowly past the warm brick of the house, the whitewashed converted stables the Doctor used as a surgery, the shrubbery and kitchen garden. He could just see the stewponds from the road.

There was a crowd of people by the stews. Dan saw the Doctor, grim and grey and lanky, standing like a heron looking down into the water. Beside him, on his knees, was young Harry Barnett the water-keeper. There were two uniformed policemen and four other men; the others, though in plain clothes, were just as unmistakably policemen as the uniformed bobbies. Two of the plain-clothes men were on their knees. All of them were looking down into the water.

Dan blinked. What in God's name could bring a squad of police to inspect a stewpond full of trout? A corpse? Was it a murderer the bloodhounds had been chasing?

Dan wanted to know what they were looking at, and he wanted to speak to Dr Smith. He dumped his bicycle, climbed through the fence, tugged off his cap, fixed his bashful yokel grin on his face, and approached the group by the stews.

He got near enough to see down into the water. It was the most horrible sight he had ever seen. It was murder, all right, and to Dan's mind quite as bad as the murder of a man.

Thousands of fish lay floating belly-up in the stewponds. Every fish in the ponds was dead.

Had a factory somewhere upstream spilled a lot of poisonous chemical into the river? No. There was no factory upstream – there was nothing except farmland, and above that empty down-land. And the main river was all right – Dan had seen healthy little grayling darting and weaving under the bridge.

It was only here, then. A mass slaughter of fish, just these fish and no others. A deliberate crime, else why the police?

Why police, anyway, for a pondful of dead trout? So many police, looking so grim? Had they brought out bloodhounds to chase a man who poisoned a few fish?

One of the detectives looked up, saw Dan, gave a start. Dan recognized him, all too clearly. He was a Sergeant, a middle-aged tough with a big white face like a Hereford bullock. He had taken Dan in for questioning, in the Milchester Police Station, two years before. Dan had been there nearly all night. The Sergeant had been very angry, and Dan had been more scared than he allowed himself to seem. Neither of them would forget it, or forget each other. It had followed a spot of bother in the Medwell Court pheasant preserves. They hadn't pinned anything on to Dan, but they'd come very, very close to it. Dan's palms were still moistened by the memory. The Hereford bullock Sergeant was the last man he wanted to see, here or anywhere, now or at any time.

'Ah,' said the Sergeant. He made a grunt not like a bullock but like a very large Hereford bull. 'This yere's the biggest villain unhung. Poach anything as soon as look at it. Proberly thought he could net un all out an' flog un in Milchester market. Shall us take him in, sir?'

'Yes,' said a man with a sharp red face like a dog-fox. 'Take him in and throw the book at him.'

3

There was a long and horrible silence. Everybody looked at Dan, then down at the obscene, pathetic, belly-up bodies of the dead fish, then up at Dan again.

The Hereford bullock Sergeant started towards Dan, moving ponderously.

'Don't be absurd,' said Dr Smith suddenly.

The Doctor was a man Dan trusted, as far as he trusted anybody. Dan trusted him to give the right advice about his mother. In a more general way, Dan was inclined to trust anybody who cast a dry fly as beautifully as the Doctor did. It wasn't logical, but it seemed in the order of things – a man who could throw a line like that must be on the side of the angels.

'I've known Mallett for years,' said the Doctor. 'His mother's a patient of mine, and he's done odd jobs here.'

'That's all very fine, Doctor,' began the foxy-faced man, whom Dan did not trust.

'Just a minute, Superintendent,' said the Doctor.

Dan goggled slightly. A Detective Superintendent, or likely a Chief Superintendent, was a powerful high-ranking officer. It was a heavy load of brass for dead fish. Was there more to this than dead fish?

But the Doctor was not abashed by the Superintendent's rank. Like many professional men Dan had known in his days in the bank, the Doctor had the habit of authority. It came of telling poor mortals what was best for them. Lawyers were the same, architects, surveyors, sometimes parsons, but doctors were the most godlike because people were frightened when they talked to them.

Dr Smith went on, 'If Mallett had killed my fish last night, he'd scarcely put his head into this hornets' nest this morning. He may be audacious but he's not suicidal.'

' 'Scuse me, sir,' said young Harry Barnett, the keeper. Harry looked glum, as he always did. He was famous for his misery. He had something to be extra miserable about today. He began to murmur to the Doctor and the foxy Superintendent, both of whom listened intently. Dan tried but failed to hear what he was saying. The Doctor was looking at the dead trout. Harry looked from the trout to Dan. The Superintendent stared fixedly at Dan, as though wanting to be sure he remembered the biggest villain unhung, who poached anything as soon as look at it.

After Harry had finished his mumbling, the Doctor said, 'This is your pigeon, Superintendent, but my keeper has convinced me.'

The Superintendent nodded, without expression, keeping his little cold eyes on Dan's face. He said, 'Where were you at five-thirty this morning, Mallett?'

Dan stared back at him, opening his eyes wide, letting his jaw sag, giving himself a moronic expression. He took his voice and manner as far as possible away from the bank, as far as possible into a cosy, antique world of smock-frocks and home-brew and haywains. In a low, treacly voice he said, 'A-ben sleepen in m'bed, zurr, 'tel cock d'crow for dawnen. M'Mam, she d'know a-ben abed, zurr, for she ben wakeful as a vixen. 'Tes the pain, a-b'lieves. A-ben wishful for t'zee you, Doctor zurr.'

'About your mother's arthritis?'

'Ay.'

'Good. Come to the surgery at 6.'

Dan nodded, saucer-eyed, screwing up his cap in his hands as though it was wet and he was trying to wring it out.

They let him go away, unimpeded, to Sir George Simpson's. He wondered what Harry Barnett had said.

The Simpsons' grass was very dry. Cutting it was light work with the machines. The mower's grass-box took a long time to fill, and the clippings from the whole lawn hardly filled a barrow. The only time-consuming thing was pulling out the croquet hoops and putting them back in the right places.

Dan knocked off at 1 and went to the Chestnut Horse, known locally, without humorous intention, as the Chestnut Arse.

' 'Mornin', stranger,' said Ted Goldingham the landlord. 'How's the old lady keepin'?'

'Fairish,' said Dan. 'Her spirit's high but her legs do wobble.'

He drank a pint of bitter and waited for Harry Barnett, who always came in at dinner-time, no matter what he was doing on the river. He could have gone home, but he and his wife hadn't spoken for three years. No one knew what the row was about. It was amazing how they managed, living together in a four-roomed cottage.

Harry came in at twenty past. His face was as lugubrious as always, not surprising considering his arrangements and considering the state of his stewponds. Harry and Dan had been at school together in the village, before Dan went on to higher things. They remained friends. Each appreciated that the other was a loner; they respected each other's privacy. Dan never asked Harry about his wife, and Harry never asked Dan what he scooped out of the stewponds, after nightfall, with the Doctor's own landing-net.

Dan said he'd backed a winner at Bath races, in the betting-shop in Milchester. He bought Harry a large gin and Dubonnet.

After a third drink Harry unbuttoned. The Doctor had had a letter that seemed to upset him. He told Harry to keep an extra close eye on the stewponds, and he went to the police. Harry did not see the letter, and the Doctor did not tell him what was in it. Harry was curious, naturally. He talked to old Nora Boakes, the Doctor's housekeeper.

'Nora says summat peculiar's goin' on,' said Harry. 'An' I agreed.'

'I agree, too,' said Dan.

31

'Ay. So Nora an' me, we both been lookin' an' listenin'. Yesterday dinner-time there came a call for Doctor on the telephone. Not a patient, Nora says, nor yet a friend. She could tell by the way Doctor talked. Soon's he finish the call, Nora says, he rings the police. He says, "Yewstop Lane, 4 o'clock tomorrer mornin', an' I stops by the road-sign for the S-bend." '

'It was him in that car,' murmured Dan.

' 'Twas him in his car. Went out at ha' pas' three, Nora says. Went to Yewstop Lane, seemin'ly, but I dunno why.'

'The police knew he was going there.'

'Sure-lee.'

'He went to meet a bloke. The police tried to catch the bloke.'

'Sure-lee. But the bloke were a sly one. He lost the dogs in Willie Martin's muck.'

'What happened to the fish, Harry? Was it poison?'

'Aye. The police took samples o' the water to analyse. The bastards put it in the drain, where we gets our flow from the river. They had a lump of chemical, likely, like a stable salt-lick, dissolvin' steady, goin' all the way through me chain o' ponds.'

'No footprints?'

'The ground's next kin to concrete, this dry weather.'

'You weren't guarding the fish?'

'No. Doctor said there weren't no call.'

'When were they poisoned?'

'Must ha' been just after first light. Five, five-thirty.'

'But why?'

'Ah. When I found the fish, I found a letter by the stew. When they put the poison in, they left the letter, in a plastic bag like a parkin'-ticket.'

'You got the letter, Harry?'

'Police took un.'

'But you saw it?'

'Ay. Said, "You had this comin', 'cause you didn't heed the warnin'. We told you not to go to the law, but you been and went. It's no good payin' the money," the letter says, "if you goes to the law. You been warned," the letter says, "so it's all your fault." '

'It's a mite vicious,' said Dan. 'By the way, what was it you told them?'

'Me?'

'The Doctor and the bloke like a fox.'

'Him they call the Super. Ah! I said it was never you poisoned the stewponds.'

'Thanks, Harry.'

'I said, "He likes a nice two-pounder, Dan Mallett does, once a week or thereabouts, for his Mam's supper." I said, "I knowed for years, but I never managed to ketch him." I said, "He'd never poison all them fish, Dan Mallett wouldn't, 'cause he wants 'em healthy for his Mam's supper." '

'Oh' said Dan. 'Is that what you said?'

'Ay. So that's why they let you go.'

Harry Barnett went off tipsily to mourn his fish. Dan went back to finish Sir George Simpson's grass.

At 6 Dan went to Dr Smith's. He sat in the waiting-room, reading an article in an ancient magazine about adding a patio to his house, until Dr Smith called him into the surgery.

He sat down, embarrassed, torturing his cap in his hands. Dr Smith knew now that the Mallett family had eaten a good many of his fat rainbows. Harry Barnett had meant well, no doubt of that, and his argument was convincing, no doubt of that either. But it was embarrassing nonetheless to sit facing Dr Smith's grim grey face.

'I trusted you, Mallett,' said the Doctor, speaking more in anger than in sorrow.

'Ay,' said Dan cautiously. He kept to the broad, slow rural voice which he used on the local gentry. ' 'Tes powerful hard t'tempt me Mam's fancy. She d'play wi' her food, mos' times. 'Tes worryen.'

'Hm. Well, we'll leave that subject for the moment. But I

haven't forgotten. Nor have the police. How is your mother?'

'Poor-lee, an' getten poorlier,' said Dan.

Dr Smith told Dan to take his mother, with a letter, to the consultant at the County Hospital. Dan explained the problem about public wards, odd-coloured nurses, and uncaring doctors who prodded and sneered.

'This is all prejudice,' said Dr Smith crossly.

'No, 'tes stark terror,' said Dan.

'What can either of us do, you or I? It's an operation in the hospital, or it's pain and disablement. The choice is your mother's, but what other alternative is there?'

'There's other hospitals. More respectful, like.'

'Private rooms? Are you talking about going to a specialist in private practice? The facility exists, of course, but the money involved – '

'C'd you write me down a name, Doctor zurr?'

Dr Smith shrugged. He wrote down a resplendent name, a Harley Street address, a telephone number. Mallett could enquire about costs. Having done so, he and his mother would be forced back to the National Health Service and the County Hospital. The old woman would have to suffer the indignities of the public wards, as thousands did. It was suffer them, or suffer pain and immobility. There *was* no other choice. The sooner these funny little people faced it, the better. Dr Smith was not hard-hearted, but he sometimes had to make himself feel so.

He was angry at the thought of all the big rainbows he might have caught on his tiny, delicate dry fly.

Dan bicycled home, to the crazy little cottage on the edge of Priory Wood. He loved it, for all its pokiness, for all his mother's yearning to live a dainty suburban life among privet hedges. It suited him as it had once suited the Priory gamekeeper. The Priory hadn't had a keeper for a long time, not since the family ran out of money, the estate was broken up, and the big house was sold. Fred Mortimer now had quite a lot of the land, and the house was a girls' school. A syndicate had the shooting, which was no good at all. Dan did quite well out of the members.

Dan put his bicycle in the shed, carefully, because one of his pedigree Blue Marble bantam hens was sitting on a dozen eggs in the corner. He had to be careful about walking out of the shed, too, because the other bantams crowded round his feet, clucking or cheeping, asking for their corn. A fortnight-old chick jumped on to the toe of Dan's boot, peeping like a tiny mechanical toy; it already had silvery, feathery trousers right down its legs to its feet. A hen called Gloria hopped on to Dan's shoulder, and murmured into his ear that she wanted to be fed first. She always was.

When Dan had got the bantams out from under his feet, he climbed up into his pigeon loft to feed the blue-laced Satinettes. He was depressed, as always, by the inadequacy of the loft, and he knew his little stud of pigeons was a third-rate lot. He intended to start all over again, and he had clear-cut long range plans.

He wondered what to say to his mother about the Harley Street specialist. The idea of a private room in a nursing-home might make a big difference to her attitude to the operation. The next thing was to get an idea of the cost. He decided to say nothing about it until he knew a bit more.

He wondered why Dr Smith, of all people, had taken his car at a walking pace down Yewstop Lane at 4 in the morning, having told the police about it. Apparently he had paid some money, but because he talked to the police, and the police had brought out bloodhounds, somebody poisoned his trout. It made no sense at all. It was not like anything Dan had ever met. Why poison trout because somebody gets chased by bloodhounds? Especially as it was not the villain, if it was a villain, but Dan who was chased by the hounds.

There was a lot of talk in the village about the dead trout. It was all speculation and rumour. Dr Smith refused to say anything to anybody. The police kept their lips buttoned, too. The *Milchester Argus* had an item about it. They said the police were pursuing investigations.

The members of the fishing syndicate were very sick. Harry Barnett told Dan that one of the syndicate wanted part of his subscription refunded, since there weren't so many fish to catch. Dan heard without surprise that this was Fred Mortimer. He was voted down by the other members, including Sir George Simpson, Major March and Admiral Jenkyn. Dan thought Fred had a point. It was certainly typical of him to try to get his money back.

And then, three days later, Fred's own hay-barn was burned.

4

Dan heard about it when he was gently proceeding with another odd job.

He had been remaking the fence, between garden and paddock, since dinner-time. It was easy and pleasant work, with something to show for it. It paid well, too.

'Time for a cup of tea, Dan,' called Mrs Calloway, crossing the lawn from the house with a mug on a tray.

Dan straightened, took half a dozen three-inch nails out of his mouth, and said, 'A-be walcome, ma'am. A drap o' tay to a tharzty chap be loik a grummet to a titmouse.'

His voice was at its deepest and slowest, his accent at its broadest. He spoke in a parody of archaic rural Wessex.

Mrs Calloway's face was puzzled but interested. She was a thin woman, approaching sixty, wife of a chartered accountant. They had bought Woodbines early in the year, for Mr Calloway's imminent retirement. The great attraction was the garden – three acres, on several levels, of well-drained greensand. Mr Calloway was a passionate gardener, and the house in suburban Ruislip had never given him scope. Here he had slaved all spring and summer, spent nearly £6,000, and had already achieved what promised to be the show garden of the neighbourhood.

Woodbines itself was two farm cottages knocked together to form a poky but picturesque house. Dan had been involved with the conversion; he knew there was enough wrong with it to keep him busy as an odd-job man for years. He was a godsend to Mrs Calloway, as everyone had told her he would be. 'Get on to Dan,' her new neighbours had said, 'he can turn his hand to everything.' And so he could. Not only that – he was a delight to have about the place, full of amusing quirks and wry local proverbs and country lore.

Mrs Calloway had never really lived in the country before, not the proper country. She liked it very much, although she faced the winter with nervousness. She was anxious to learn about her new world – its traditional crafts, the old customs and names, the real life of the countryside unseen by visitors. She had several eager tutors among women whose husbands had retired some years previously, but her favourite source was Dan.

'A grummet to a titmouse,' she repeated. 'What exactly is a grummet, Dan?'

'Tha taks a mossel o' beef suet,' explained Dan, who had just invented the word, 'an' tha threads a bit o' twine a'through un, an' tha hangs un where tha can zees un, for to make a mummery-show, loik. Titmice d'cam for to gobble un, a-perchen an' a-pecken an' covorten, 'tes stimmilent for t'watch un.'

Mrs Calloway nodded. She would remember the quaint old word 'grummet', and bring it out casually during local coffee-mornings; she would remember, too, to hang up a lump of suet for the tits in the winter.

Dan was the biggest of many surprises of living at Medwell Fratrorum. He was like something, she told her husband, left behind by the receding waters of history – a relic, still vigorous, of much earlier times, caught in this isolated rock-pool. Some of the other country folk, like her daily and the people in the village shop, talked with pretty broad accents, and used a few unfamiliar words, but none was in Dan's class. Yet he was not old. No one knew his exact age, which was occasionally a subject of speculation at local dinner-parties: but he could not have been more than thirty-five. His untidy mouse-coloured hair showed no trace of grey; his eyes were a clear, childlike blue, direct and innocent, utterly disarming; his face had probably been leathery and crumpled from an early age, owing to being out in all weathers at all hours.

38

Dan put down his hammer, tugged off his cap, and took the tray from Mrs Calloway. Beside the mug of tea there were five lumps of sugar, some ginger biscuits and a slice of walnut cake. Dan grunted his appreciation, and squatted down under a purple-tufted buddleia, which smelled of honey and attracted butterflies. He made Mrs Calloway think of a leveret.

Yes, she thought, pleased with the countryside metaphor, Dan was a leveret as he crouched with the tea-tray under the honey-scented spikes of blossom, he was shy yet trusting, wild yet reassuring. But there was nothing animal about him. He was a strange man, an unfamiliar type, almost like a foreigner – but he was very much a man. Those blue eyes! Those strong, narrow brown hands! Even after a hard day in the hot sun, he did not give off the acrid, sweaty smell which made Mr Calloway revolting after an hour's gentle pruning. Mrs Calloway guessed pruriently that Dan was a devil with the girls. If she herself had been twenty years younger, or even only ten years younger . . .

Dan was thinking that fifteen minutes was a reasonable time to spend on his tea. That amount of his time would cost Mrs Calloway fifty pence. It was a fine way to earn money, eating ginger biscuits under a butterfly-bush. This job was highly profitable altogether. He had abstracted the fence-rails from a pile of planking brought by the builder who did the conversion, and hidden them in the spinney beside the paddock. He was charging ten pence a foot, which was cheap. Forty yards of fence with three rails made £36. His labour was £2 an hour, which compared favourably with rates in Ruislip. He had offered to throw in three-inch nails, which also came from the builder, but Mrs Calloway insisted on paying for them. Dan was not impressed by this open-handedness. People came from London and thought they could buy popularity. The Calloways were natural victims.

Mrs Calloway took the tea-tray. Dan returned to the fence. As he worked, he compared what he was doing to the sort of thing he might have been doing a dozen years earlier. The thought made his hammer pound so merrily that the fence would be finished in no time. That wouldn't do. He slowed up.

He heard the crunch of a horse's feet on the gravel of the drive. He looked up, taking the nails out of his mouth. The horse came into view, round the corner of the drive by a clump of lilacs. Dan knew the horse but not the rider. The horse was a fat grey called Cherry, almost white in her old age, belonging to the Hadfield sisters, and hired to their most nervous and inexperienced customers. The rider was a girl in her middle twenties, strangely dressed in jeans, bikini top, and hunting-cap. She was slim but not thin; her face was round and very pretty and pink-gold from the sun; she had long fair hair. Dan inspected with unconcealed interest her bare golden midriff and shoulders, and the shape of her breasts in the bikini.

He hurried over to hold Cherry's head. He knew it was quite unnecessary to hold the head of such a sleepy old thing; he also knew the Hadfield sisters would never have hired her to anybody who could ride.

He looked up at the rider with open admiration and a slight, quizzical smile. He said, insincerely, in his best banker's voice, 'I can see you've ridden much better horses than this one.'

'Not many,' she said. 'But I had a very nice wooden one when I was small.' She smiled. She seemed suddenly conscious of how little she was wearing about the waist.

She dismounted awkwardly. She said, 'Ooh, I'm stiff.'

She was exactly the same height as Dan. Her jeans were tight and her figure excellent. The stretch of golden skin between jeans and bikini top looked wonderfully smooth and warm and welcoming. Dan gulped. Few tummies as nice as this one had ever come his way.

The girl patted the old pony's neck. 'They said I could keep him here tonight and ride him back in the morning.'

'She'll have to go in the shed,' said Dan. 'The paddock isn't railed yet. Would you like me to untack her?'

'Do what?'

'Take off the saddle and bridle.'

'Oh yes. Would you very kindly? I might undo the wrong buckles.'

Dan liked the fact that she didn't pretend to know any more about horses than she knew: this made her exceptional among most of the nobs in the area and all the Miss Hadfields' customers. He liked many things about her, which he could see or guess at. He wondered who she was.

At this moment Mrs Calloway came out of the house carrying a handful of money.

'Oh there you are, Camilla,' she called. 'Have a nice ride? What a nice white pony. Have you met Dan Mallett, who does *everything* for *everybody* round here? This is our daughter-in-law, Dan, married to our son David. She's staying with us for a few days while David is abroad.'

Everything for everybody? thought Camilla, glancing at Dan.

She had not expected problems in this remote and sleepy part of the country. Avoiding problems was one of the reasons for coming here. She had never found temptation easy to resist, or 'no' easy to say. This was partly politeness, she told herself. It was also partly because saying 'yes' could be so intensely enjoyable. She had thought she would not have occasion to say 'no' in Medwell Fratrorum, under the beady eyes of the in-laws. She had thought there'd be nothing but ancient wrinklies, and yokels smelling of drains. London was full of hazards, of old boy-friends and new ones. While David was abroad, London was tiger country. It was tiger country even when he was at home, since the marriage was becoming distinctly disillusioned and rancorous.

No temptations, down here among the turnips and things? Those big baby-blue eyes? That tuft of hair sticking out at the back of his head?

Shocked not by the direction in which her mind was working, but a bit shocked at the speed at which it was travelling, Camilla turned, blushing, to her mother-in-law.

She said, 'We passed the most ghastly fire. A huge barn, roaring like mad. I suppose it was hay. Would it be hay? Two fire-engines were there, but I don't think they did much good.'

'Where?' asked Dan, still holding Cherry's head.

'Just the other side of the village, a vast barn with a metal roof but no sides, by itself near some trees.'

'Fred Mortimer's,' said Dan. 'He had fifty tons of hay in that barn, more than two thousand quids' worth.'

Mrs Calloway looked at him, her eyebrows raised in surprise.

Dan added, in his broadest accent, for her benefit, 'Mas'r Mortimer d'grow a zoight o' hay for t'sell come turn o' the year. They varment schoolboys a-ben a-smoken there, a-b'lieves.'

'I expect so,' said Mrs Calloway vaguely.

It was evident to Dan that a disaster which did not strike herself was not really a disaster. Dan put this in a pocket of his mind with the mushroom-coloured fitted carpets the Calloways had in the house, with Mrs Calloway's blue-rinsed hair, with their white-painted wrought-iron garden furniture. To him all these things somehow spoke of tax evasion, fiddled expense accounts, and cases of cut-price gin bought on the firm's account. He knew it was not logical to make a moral judgement on the basis of the colour of someone's carpet. He did it just the same. It was in the order of things, like trusting Dr Smith because he cast a fly so beautifully.

He glanced at the girl. She was now looking at him in astonishment. He realized this was the accent, the picturesque yokel performance. He had used, to the girl, the voice of Grammar School and bank. He winked at her. This was risky, perhaps, but it was a quick way of finding out a bit more about her. She giggled. He immediately knew quite a lot more about her.

She said to Mrs Calloway, 'Aren't you playing bridge this afternoon, Mildred?'

'Yes, dear. I must leave the very minute I've changed. Here you are, Dan.' She handed him the money. 'This is for another two hours, of course. I'm *trusting* you. But I know I can do that.'

Reverting once again to his treacliest accent, and glancing at the girl to include her in the joke, Dan said, 'A-do ondertak', ma'am, t'bang a fist o' they zhinen nails en amonst thik railens. Ay! 'At a-do.'

Dan pocketed his wages and the cost of his timber, and led Cherry to the shed. He untacked her, put the saddle across a beam with the irons tucked up under the flaps, and hung the bridle on a nail. He gave Cherry a bucket of water. She'd do very well without a feed. Had she been sweating at all he would have rubbed her down, but she had probably not been out of a walk. She looked at him with apathetic affection, having known him all her life. Dan was fond of her, but she was not an interesting horse.

Mrs Calloway was driving off in her car when Dan came back from the shed. Camilla was on the lawn, pretending to inspect the new fence.

Dan said, in the accents of the Milchester bank, 'I wonder if I could make a telephone call?'

'Yes, of course. Come in.'

Dan wiped his boots with elaborate care, and followed her on to the mushroom fitted carpet of the hall. She led him past the open door of the dining-room, which had a quantity of silver laid out on a sideboard, and into the sunny drawing-room.

'There you are,' the girl said. 'Help yourself. I'll go and get a bit more decent.'

'Please don't,' said Dan, giving her the grin that had worked so well so often.

She blushed. It suited her. She was not really sophisticated.

She went out, shutting the door, and Dan telephoned the Harley Street specialist. He spoke to a receptionist, who put him through to a secretary. He used his bank voice, his blue-suit-and-black-shoes voice, his scampi-by-candlelight voice. He mentioned Dr Smith's name and recommendation.

'My present concern,' he said in the voice of the bank, 'is to get a general idea of the cost. Simply the area. I realize you can't commit yourself, and I am not asking you to do so. But I am anxious for general guidance, you understand, to help us make plans.'

'Certainly, Mr Mallett.'

The general idea of the cost was a considerable shock. The surgeon's fee, for the operation on both hips, would be in the region of £500. The anaesthetist would be additional, perhaps £80. Hospitalization would be not less than fifteen days, probably eighteen or twenty for an elderly woman patient. Private rooms in suitable clinics were seldom less than £25 a day, exclusive of drugs, X-ray, physiotherapy and the like. Rooms could go up to £60 a day and more.

Dan did a calculation on a pad by the telephone, with the deftness he had learned at the bank and never forgotten.

'Not much change,' he said, 'out of £1,200.'

'No,' agreed the secretary coolly. 'You should budget on a figure at least as high as that.'

Dan hung up slowly. There were three choices, then. The public ward and the sneering doctors. The pain going on and getting worse. Or finding £1,200.

The decision made itself.

He stood up and crossed the room softly. He could hear footsteps upstairs – the girl was still making herself decent, or indecent, or something. He crossed the hall and went into the dining-room. He had a look at the silver on the sideboard. He knew a little about silver from his days at the bank – clients had included the principal Milchester auctioneers and a firm of silversmiths and jewellers. The candlesticks were early Victorian Sheffield plate, much more valuable than they would have been a few years before. The salvers had only bullion value. The cigarette box was ugly but massive. Six little pepperpots looked really good – Dan thought, remembering with difficulty what he had picked up on the subject, that they were George II.

Would he come for them all, one windy night? It was too soon to say. He had not made his mind up about the Calloways. Instinct told him they deserved it. The old woman didn't care a farthing about Fred Mortimer's hay. That went with her blue hair, and the mushroom carpets, and the wrought-iron furniture. But it wasn't logical and it might be unfair. It was too soon to say.

He might leave the Calloways alone. But they, or people like them, were his only source of £1,200. In some ways it was turning out a pity he'd ever left the bank.

He was outside the house when the daughter-in-law came downstairs. She had changed into a skimpy cotton dress. Her legs were bare. They were nice legs.

'All right?' she said.

'Yes, thank you,' said Dan. 'It was very kind of you to let me use the telephone.'

'Not at all. Any time. Feel free.'

She might mean much or little by that. Dan didn't wait to find out. He went straight back to the fence, and began banging in nails like a triphammer. She looked at him a little forlornly, he thought. She was probably lonely. The old Calloways wouldn't be very good company for a girl like her, nor the young one from what Dan had seen. But if he was going to raise £1,200, he must stay clear of involvement with the people he was raising it from. That was a matter of conscience and prudence: some of each.

If he had a new career he must be professional about it.

5

Dan bicycled home through a perfect evening.

The mown hayfields, sad and yellow for some time, were showing patches of green again. There were clumps of misty-blue harebells at their edges, but most of the wildflowers were fading. Swifts were wheeling and screaming over the water-meadows near the village: Dan tried to distinguish the young birds learning to fly from their parents. Staring up at them, as he bicycled, he nearly went into the ditch. The oats and barley were fading from green to silver, the wheat turning to gold. Hordes of sparrows were attacking the ripening grain, rising in noisy clouds as Dan bicycled by. There were plenty of part-ridges, too, far more than a few years previously.

Dan pondered about this as he pedalled slowly between patchy thorn hedges. He thought partridges liked insects best, especially caterpillars and crawly bugs, though he had watched them eat grain and seeds and spring wheat and even grass. It was less spraying that made the difference to the partridges, less mur-derous insecticide. A good job too. Dan sometimes thought he liked roast partridge even better than pheasant.

As he went by, a covey of a dozen got up from the corner of a rootfield – two parents, the rest half-grown cheepers. They were all on the ground again after a few yards, completely hidden. Dan made a note of the place. Just before sunrise, using the hedgerows, he could get there without anybody seeing him. The young birds could fly, but not very well yet. They were much smaller than the adults. It would be worth waiting an-other three weeks or so, to let them fatten up, before bringing out the net and the old pointer. There was no point in leaving plump young birds for the guns.

Dan's way took him past Mortimer's big outlying hay-barn. Young Mrs Calloway was right – the hay must have roared like hell. It was beautiful hay, too – enough rain in the spring to give it plenty of bottom and a high weight to the acre, a fine fortnight for the harvest. They reckoned it forty-eight bales to the ton. Fred Mortimer could get a pound a bale now, and it might be twice that in February if there was a hard winter. It was all gone. What wasn't burned was drenched with water from the fire hoses; it would rot and blacken and smell musty, and the hungriest animals would hardly look at it.

Who'd do a trick like that?

It could have been the village boys, with matches or burning glasses, either by mistake or because bonfires were exciting.

It couldn't be malice. Some people, yes. Willie Martin, perhaps. But not Fred Mortimer. It was a tramp, a gipsy, a drunk, a schoolboy. An accident. Nobody would own up. No doubt Fred was insured.

Fred might not be loser financially, but he'd be very angry. Like a lot of successful men, Fred had a violent temper. It was part of forcefulness, of drive. Losing your temper was a help to crashing through opposition. Fred's farmhands might suffer a bit as a result of this holocaust; his household would suffer more, his two boys and the housekeeper.

The housekeeper was old Glad Fowler, who looked like a weasel and sounded like something out of Domesday Book. She didn't know it, but she'd been very useful to Dan. When he used his most antique rural voice to beguile the local nobs, it was Glad he imitated. Poor old thing – if Fred shouted with rage, it was likely to break Glad in half, just from the impact of the noise. Fred's house couldn't be the easiest billet for an old bundle of twigs like her. There was plenty of work to do and not much fun to be had. Musing about old Glad, it seemed to Dan that he had never heard her laugh, or seen her so much as smile. He had known her all his life. No smile in thirty-five years. She was as miserable as young Harry Barnett, and with even more reason.

Two mornings later Dan got out his best blue suit, the one he had worn to the bank. He polished up and put on his pointed black banker's shoes. He put on a white shirt and a dark tie. He plastered down his unruly hair with water.

His mother looked at him wistfully, all dressed up as a banker.

He said, 'I'm going in to Milchester on the bus.'

'Lookin' for a job?' she said.

'In a manner of speaking. Yes, you could say that.'

She nodded, hoping but not trusting him. His father had sometimes talked of getting a job. It never went much beyond talk.

Dan got off the bus in the Market Square. He walked to West Street and to an antique shop called The Box of Delights. The shop had been a client of the bank, and Dan had known the proprietor well. There was something fishy about him. He had never been in trouble, as far as Dan knew, but the business had a turnover far bigger than the shop looked as if it could possibly have. The owner, Mr Prior, used to come to the bank with big bundles of cash. He drew big bundles of cash, too. He said he was buying stock. No doubt he was, but Dan had wondered what stock he was buying, where it came from, who it went to.

The window contained, as it always had, a jumble of dusty rubbish. Dan pushed the door open, jangling a bell. A middle-aged woman with a lantern jaw came out of the back of the shop; she was artily dressed, and her hair was bound round with a green chiffon bandeau.

'Mr Prior available?' said Dan, in his best banker's manner.

'Oh no,' said the woman. 'Mr Prior has had no connection here for two years. I am his successor.'

'Ah. I didn't know. What became of Mr Prior?'

'He's retired. I think he lives abroad.'

'I'm glad he can afford it.'

'Oh, he can afford it all right. Oh yes.'

The suggestion was that the odd-looking woman knew about Mr Prior, and that Dan's guess had been right. Even without Mr Prior, The Box of Delights was probably the right place to come to.

Dan said he was Mr Harry Barnett. He was interested in selling a number of items of silver, some antique. 'But I don't want them sold or put on display locally,' he said.

The woman stared at him. Then she looked away. She said casually, 'Why not, Mr Barnett?'

'I don't want my friends to know I'm broke.'

The woman laughed. She said, 'Actually it's not an unusual request. I am sometimes asked to dispose of things, er, discreetly. What I generally do is put them in a sale a long way from here. Some big provincial sale-room where things go in and out quickly. Continental dealers very often buy, so there's no fear of an item turning up in your neighbour's house.'

'That sounds,' said Dan, as casual as she, 'just the ticket. I'll bring the stuff in next time I come.'

'*Do. Do.* Can you give me an idea of what's involved?'

Dan described the Calloways' silver as well as he could.

'I'm not yet quite sure if it will be that lot or quite a different lot,' he said. 'In any case, I'm sure I shall be obliged to sell quite a lot of other things in the near future.'

'All silver?'

'Oh no.' Dan thought about the contents of Sir George Simpson's house, of Admiral Jenkyn's, of Mr and Mrs Potter's at the Old Mill, of Major March's at Medwell Court. 'There might be pictures. Antique weapons. Clocks. What would you say to jewellery?'

'I can certainly handle jewellery.'

They shook hands, and parted on the friendliest terms.

Dan wondered if the arty woman was wise to him. It seemed likely. He thought she was deliberately shutting her mind to awkward questions. He looked and sounded respectable. That was enough for her: that was her excuse if anything turned sour. She couldn't be accused by the law of anything worse than gullibility.

If she bought the business from Prior, she was probably one of Prior's kidney. She'd be discreet. That was all Dan required of her – that and the money for the old lady's operation.

Dan went back to the Market Square, and into the Red Lion. He went to the writing-room, and wrote a careful and correct letter to the Harley Street specialist. He explained his mother's physical and mental condition, and asked for an appointment in two months' time. He thought he would have some money by then.

He bought a stamp from the hotel receptionist, and posted the letter in the hall. Then he made for the saloon bar, a choice dictated by the way he was dressed. His way took him past the open door of a room called the Vintners' Lounge, which had hunting prints, coach horns, an expensive cold buffet, and wine by the glass.

Dan was not at all surprised to see Fred Mortimer standing at the bar.

Fred had a big round red face, something between a harvest moon and a Jersey cow. He was the richest farmer in half a dozen parishes round Medwell Fratrorum. He was very sociable and jolly. His booming voice could be heard, shouting jokes and greetings, at every kind of local fête and function, parish meetings, old folks' outings, children's parties, Guy Fawkes bonfires. He was a familiar figure in Milchester, too, being on the Rural District Council, buying and selling at the local market and the horse-sales, doing business with banks and solicitors and a local stockbroker. Fred's hay had been burned earlier in the week. Probably the insurance people had been out to see the mess, and he was in to see them. Nobody knew, as far as Dan had heard, how the fire started.

Although Fred was a local farmer, it was no surprise to see him in the flossy exclusive lounge of the Red Lion. If Fred had a weakness, it was that he was a bit of a snob, like his daughter. He liked being seen in public with the Sirs and Colonels of the area. When he came to village doings like the old folks' outings, he came like a sort of old-time squire. He wore tweedy clothes and a gold watch-chain. To Dan's mind it was harmless; Fred was entitled to act half-way like gentry.

Fred was drinking gin at the bar with a group of local nobs. They probably, thought Dan, called Fred 'the salt of the earth' when they talked to each other.

'Agri-something,' Fred was booming, his cheery voice reaching to every corner of the pub. 'I never heard of it myself.'

'Nor I,' said a city gent camouflaged in tweeds, unknown to Dan personally but deeply familiar as a type.

There was a chorus of negative grunts from the other nobs. None of them had heard of Fred's Agri-something.

'What did you do when you got the letter?' asked one of them.

'Nothing,' said Fred. 'What would *you* do? I thought it was a joke, or a madman. I tore it up. Then, a day or two later, up goes my hay like a ruddy torch. You tell me, gents, is that a bloody coincidence?'

'You've been to the police now, surely?'

'That I have.'

One of the group, an elderly thin brown man, began to talk about agrarian outrages in India in the 'thirties. The parallels seemed close. The conversation drifted to terrorists and the need for firm measures. Dan hung about in the passage, as inconspicuous as one of the brass warming-pans on the wall: but he heard nothing more of interest.

He thought about it on the bus going home.

The Doctor had had a letter which upset him. He did something that somebody didn't like, which was going to the police, so his trout were killed. Fred Mortimer had had a letter from Agri-something. He ignored it. He lost £2,000 worth of hay.

It was all very odd. What was Agri-something after? Dan could understand doing things for profit – snaring a pheasant, nicking a silver candlestick – but destruction was pointless. Where was the profit from dead trout or burned hay? What could Agri-something be about?

'You get the job?' asked old Mrs Mallett.

'Could be. The offer's there.'

'Bank?'

'No. More a sort of trading job. I haven't made up my mind.'

'I'll be bound you have, though.' The old lady sighed, her hopes dwindling.

Next day Dan was back at the Calloways', building the fence with his own rails. He did not see the daughter-in-law; he wondered if she was still there, but thought it better not to ask. The most refined people, like Mrs Calloway, often had the dirtiest and most suspicious minds. There were butterflies on the buddleia, as there should be, a Peacock and a Red Admirable, which nowadays people called a Red Admiral because they were too lazy to say the extra syllable. The Medwell grocer delivered during the morning. Young Phil Grinstead drove the van and carried in the cardboard box of Mrs Calloway's order. Young Phil was not very bright. He should have known to go to the back door. But there was no call for Mrs Calloway to talk to him as she did. He was almost in tears when he left, his broad spotty face crumpled with humiliation. He tried his best. Everybody knew that, and made allowances. But not Mrs Calloway, the grand outsider from London with blue hair and fitted mushroom-coloured carpets.

The incident tipped the scale. It decided Dan's attitude to the Calloways. His new career could begin immediately, and as planned.

Dan slipped out soon after midnight, having tucked his mother up in bed. He set off across the fields to the village.

He got to the Calloways' house about 12.45. The moon had set. There was no dew. The husband was away in London, due back tomorrow. The daughter-in-law might be there, might not. There was no dog. There were no lights on. Dan saw in the starlight that two upstairs windows were open.

Dan crossed the cherished garden to the shed where he had put old Cherry the pony. She was still there, or there again. She whickered at him; he whispered to her and stroked her fat old neck. In the lean-to beside the shed he found what he was looking for: a sack of heavy multi-ply paper which had held John Innes compost.

He went up to the walls of the house, keeping to the grass, avoiding flowerbeds and gravel. He picked a sash window at the end of the house farthest from the open bedroom windows. With the blade of his knife he eased back the catch. The catch opened with a loud click. Dan stood motionless, listening. He opened the window gently and slid into the blackness of the sitting-room. He brought the compost sack with him. He crossed the room carefully, remembering little tables with framed photographs. The door stood open into the hall. In pitch darkness Dan crossed the hall without hesitation to the door of the dining-room. It was open. He went in, leaving the door ajar behind him.

The dining-room windows gave on to the garden and paddock. They were not overlooked by any other house. Dan was safe in using his pencil flashlight. He switched it on and swung it towards the sideboard.

The room was flooded with light.

Dan turned, his heart in his mouth. He looked down the muzzle of a twelve-bore shotgun.

6

Mrs Calloway's daughter-in-law held the gun. Dan had forgotten her name – some kind of herb or flower, but not quite rightly.

'You!' she said, in a tone of utter amazement.

'You dragged me here,' said Dan, 'like a magnet.'

Her long fair hair was in girlish disarray. She wore a floor-length cotton dressing-gown. Her feet were bare.

The shotgun trembled in her hands, but its general direction was the buckle of his belt.

Dan attempted his most disarming smile, at the same time tugging off his cap.

Her face remained deadly serious. Dan realized she had guts. She was very frightened of tackling a burglar with a shotgun, but she was doing it just the same.

She said, 'So it was you. I can't believe it.'

'Me?' said Dan.

He wondered if someone had been there before him. He glanced at the sideboard. All the silver was there. The Calloways had not been burgled.

'What was me?' asked Dan.

'What are you doing with that sack?'

'This sack?' Dan looked down; he was still holding the heavy paper compost-bag; he dropped it. 'I found it in the lobby,' he said.

'Rubbish.'

'That's what I thought. Dropped in error. I tripped over it . . . What was me?'

'You wrote that letter.'

The light broke.

'Ah,' said Dan. 'Another one. But you've got nothing here like trout or hay . . .'

The gun shook in the girl's hand. Her finger was on one of the triggers. The light blazed out into the hall from the open door. Their voices might be heard all over the house. She might shoot him, on purpose or by accident. She might keep him covered and telephone the police; Dan could picture the Superintendent's fox-like mask. Mrs Calloway might hear them, or see the light. She'd know very well she never dropped a dirty old compost-sack on the hall carpet. She'd ring the police. As things stood, the best that could happen to Dan was a stretch in gaol, and the worst was a hole in the guts.

He was curious about the letter. He wanted to hear about it, if possible see it. But first things first.

'I don't know anything about a letter,' said Dan solemnly. 'I came to see you.'

'Rubbish.'

With desperate earnestness he said, 'I've been like a madman since I saw you, looking so beautiful on the pony. I've thought of nothing else except that bit of tummy above your breeches. It's the most beautiful thing I've ever seen.'

Her mouth dropped open. Dan inspected her face anxiously. It was hard to tell if she felt shock, rage or pleasure: or whether she believed a word of what he was saying.

It seemed best to keep attacking. Her husband was abroad. There'd been a crackle between them, a bit of summer lightning, when she dismounted from Cherry. She liked being looked at.

Dan said, 'I've never believed a few inches of tummy could be so beautiful. I've been half mad, wondering what the rest of you looked like. So you see, it's your fault I'm here. You dragged me here like a magnet.'

Her mouth was still open and her eyes wide. Dan could not read her expression. She was like a young rabbit caught in the headlights of a car.

The worst happened. An anxious voice called down the stairs, 'Camilla?'

That was her name. Between camomile and camellia. Dan's mother drank camomile tea. There were camellias in the garden here: they'd arrived with their roots in sacks of moist peat, and Dan dug the holes for them.

'Is anything wrong?' called Mrs Calloway from the top of the stairs.

Dan had no idea what Camilla was going to say, or what was going to happen to him. He smiled. He had four smiles: a disarming smile, a lecherous smile, a submissive smile, a masterful smile; he tried to make this one a mixture of all four.

It worked.

Camilla called, 'It's all right, Mildred. I didn't feel sleepy, so I came down for a book.'

'In the dining-room, dear?'

'I was looking for some orange squash.'

The women called good night to each other. Dan heard a door close. He felt his smile broaden into a grin of pure relief. Camilla was looking more than ever like a mesmerized rabbit; or like a plump young partridge, flat to the ground among the stubbles, held by the eye of the cross old pointer Pansy.

The gun wobbled madly in her hands. Dan stepped forward and took it from her. He glanced at the breech. It was on safe. He wondered if it was even loaded. He propped it against the wall and put his arms round Camilla's waist. She threw hers round his neck. It was then that he discovered that she had nothing on under the cotton dressing-gown.

Camilla did not think she was a bad girl. Not a very good one, but not a *very* bad one. Her appetites were normal. She liked food and drink and sunshine and moderate exercise and being made love to by very attractive men.

Nobody had embraced her passionately for some weeks. Her husband had lost interest in doing it, and she had lost interest in him doing it. He was getting more and more like his father.

This mysterious little brown man with the astonishing blue eyes had popped into her life when she least expected him, and most wanted him. All her prudence, all her good resolutions, flew away from her like the leaves of an ash-tree in a November gale. She felt much better without them. She responded joyfully to his kiss. She felt her body coming awake after weeks of reluctant sleep.

They crept upstairs hand-in-hand, and she locked the door of her bedroom.

He made love, Camilla found, cheerfully and gently. It was a delightful combination. He was not uncouth, nor smelly, nor brutal, nor boring, nor talkative, nor guilty, nor in too much of a hurry, nor concerned to prove anything. There was a kind of elegance about him, of manner as well as of body. He was not what her husband and his friends called an oik, yob or trog. It was impossible to say what he was. He was himself, in a special category which only he occupied.

She hugged him joyfully. The skin of his back was like a young girl's.

'I'm crying,' she whispered. 'Isn't that silly?'

Dan found himself moved by her tears. He knew he was sometimes sentimental, but he had not expected to feel sentimental about this girl.

Later she whispered, 'You know you've got the most beautiful blues eyes? But you're too thin. I can feel all your ribs. Does that tickle? Goodness, what muscles. You won't breathe a word about this to anybody, will you?'

'Of course not. I don't kiss and tell.'

'Some kiss . . . and I daren't have another fuss. Will you swear?'

Dan swore by muck and by molehill, an oath which he invented.

They tiptoed downstairs and into Mr Calloway's den. Camilla, her dressing-gown loosely tied, searched among the papers on her father-in-law's desk.

'I'm sure Mildred put it here . . Yes, here it is.'

It was typed on ordinary white paper. There was no sender's address. It was unsigned.

Edwin Calloway Esq,   23rd July
Woodbines,
Medwell Fratrorum,
Nr Milchester.

Dear Mr Calloway:

It has come to our attention that you have invested a great amount of time, effort and finance in the garden of your property. We understand you intend a truly magnificent garden, and take this opportunity to wish you every success with it.

As you may know, there has been a vandalism problem in this area, no doubt caused by youths from permissive or underprivileged homes. We feel obliged to point out to you that a show-place garden such as yours will be, unfortunately, an attractive target for these destructive imbeciles. We are horrified at the thought that your devoted labours and heavy financial outlay will be completely destroyed some night, perhaps by a bulldozer, a herd of cattle, or an overall spray of concentrated weedkiller.

We therefore undertake to guard your property against vandalism for an initial down-payment of £300 and £25 per week thereafter. We are sure you will agree that these charges are moderate when set against the investment you have already made and the extent of the damage the vandals would do.

We point out that discussion of this letter with the police

will greatly annoy the vandals, should they come to hear of it, with the result that the extent of the damage is likely to be that much greater. The presence of a police or other guard would also have an inflammatory effect.

The initial payment is to be in used notes of mixed denominations. You are advised to make this available immediately. Instructions for remitting will be given to you by telephone.

Assuring you of our best attention at all times,

We remain, yours very truly,

AgriSecurity.

'Ho,' said Dan at last. 'When did this come?'

'This morning.'

'What did you do?'

'Mildred rang up her husband in London. He said do nothing till he got here. That's tomorrow.'

'Have they phoned?'

'Yes. Early this evening. I took the call.'

'What did they say?'

'Nothing. They asked for Edwin. I said they'd have to ring again.'

'How did they take that?'

'I don't know. Cool. That's why I was edgy tonight.'

'What will the old man do?'

'Go to the police, I should think.'

'Hum. What kind of voice?'

'Sort of a country voice, a local voice. Not a very strong accent.'

'A man?'

'Yes. He didn't say much.'

'You might have been edgy,' said Dan, 'but you're wonderful calm about it.'

'I am now.' She giggled. 'There's nothing like it for the nerves. Anyway, they won't try anything until they've spoken to Edwin, not if they want his money.'

'But you came rushing downstairs with a gun.'

'I was lying awake. I was lonely. I was not so much edgy as itchy, actually. I heard the pony.'

'Itchy?'

'Yes.' She blushed. 'As a matter of fact I was thinking about you. That was why I was so surprised it was you in the dining-room.'

There was nothing more to be learned from the letter or from Camilla. Meanwhile her dressing-gown was loosely tied in front. Dan drew it apart. He kissed her.

'More?' she whispered.

'One for the road,' said Dan.

He kissed her good night. She shifted in the bed and murmured sleepily.

He tiptoed downstairs and went into the dining-room. He had a battle with his conscience. He would not, now, take anything from Camilla. That would be disgusting. Her property was absolutely safe from him. But the things on the sideboard weren't *her* property. These people weren't her parents, either. They weren't protected by his obligations to her. They were people who bullied poor young Phil Grinstead, when he brought the groceries to the front door.

The battle fought and won, he put all the silver from the sideboard into the compost-sack. He inspected the gun. It was loaded; he broke it and pocketed the cartridges. It was not as good as his own, but he decided to take it. It felt and smelled oily – obviously it had not been used since the previous winter. It was rather surprising Mr Calloway even possessed a sporting gun.

Dan had been careful to touch nothing inside the house except the silver, the gun, and Camilla. He was taking the silver and the gun, and they'd hardly fingerprint Camilla. He wondered if skin carried prints. Anyway she was certain to keep quiet.

He crept across the hall and the sitting-room, and went out

by the sitting-room window. He left the window open, but carefully wiped the bits of the frame he had touched. The police would spot the marks of his knife. The Calloways would fit burglar-proof window catches, but those wouldn't stop a diamond glass-cutter, if Dan ever came back for the stuff they bought with the insurance money.

He crossed the garden, climbed the fence, and set off across the fields towards home.

He thought as he went.

He had heard of something called a protection racket, but he had never met it. He had wondered how it worked. He was impressed with it. It was beautifully simple. What's more, it was easier in the country than it would be in a town, because everything was spread so wide. There was a crop here, a garden there, oil-tank, hay-barn, pigeon-loft – you couldn't put a guard on all the lot, not the police, not the farmers and householders themselves. You'd need a whole army to guard one parish, one man every quarter-acre, all night every night.

Letters had gone out to three people, that he knew of. How many more letters had gone out? How many more were going out now? How many people were there like the Calloways? The scale of the thing could be enormous. All it took was a typewriter, a ream of paper, a few stamps, and a pocketful of coppers for making calls from a box.

Also you needed one or two men. But hiring men was a drawback, a big risk, it must be. They'd know who you were and what you were doing. They'd have you by the double handful, and after a bit they'd pull. They'd ask for a bigger cut, blackmail you. Dan himself had never fancied working with anybody – never fancied being in anybody's power. He thought that whoever ran AgriSecurity had either a very big problem there, or else a very good solution.

The other problem was collecting the payments without getting nabbed while you were doing it. Used notes were fine. But how was the money handed to AgriSecurity? You had to say a time and place. That was the point the police would watch, as they did with kidnappers. They'd mark the notes, too, or take the numbers. Dan speculated about how he'd arrange it, if he was AgriSecurity. He thought of various ideas, but he doubted if any of them was proof against a discreet watch and a quick pounce.

He went along the edge of Fred Mortimer's six-acre, not far from the burned-out hay-barn. Fred had oats in the field this year. The tall crop looked silver in the starlight; it was nearly ready for the combine. The harvest was going to be a good one, if the weather held. It was a perfect time, Dan thought, for AgriSecurity to get busy. The farmers could be hit harder, with less trouble, than at any other time. They were at full stretch, with no spare labour for guarding themselves. Standing corn, ready to cut; barns full of sacks of grain; combines which could be disabled the day they were desperately needed. Fred Mortimer grew malting as well as feed barley, a terribly valuable crop. AgriSecurity had thrown a scare into him. He'd gone to the police, he said. If they burned something else, in spite of the police, would Fred begin to pay?

Thinking about that made Dan wonder how much money was involved. The Calloways weren't asked much – £100 a month, £1,200 a year. Only a garden was involved there. He cared about it, but it wasn't vital to him. A big farmer like Fred Mortimer had far more to lose, had far more invested. He could afford heavy money. He'd refused to pay, but he still might be forced to. And there was this about it, too – Fred's barn and the Doctor's trout might make a lot of people pay who would have stood out.

It was extortion by terror.

Yes, Dan thought, the money could be very good indeed. And the only real outlay was wages. Dan wondered if he himself was in the right line of business.

When Dan got home, he went not to the cottage but deep into the woods behind. There was a warren in a sandy bank under the roots of a beech tree: a small city of rabbit holes. He stowed the Calloways' silver deep in a hole, then strewed handfuls of sand to cover his tracks.

His mother was awake. He was shocked by the haggardness of her paper-white face on the pillow. He brought her a hot drink and an aspirin, but she needed much more than aspirin. She needed the operation.

The next afternoon Dan was working at the Old Mill, Mr Potter's house on the river at the edge of the village, a conversion done ten years earlier by a speculative builder from the town. The plumbing and wiring, subcontracted, were pretty good, but the carpentry was botched and the outbuildings were in a tumbledown state: consequently Dan had done a lot of odd jobs there: he knew his way about the house, and he knew everything in it. He sometimes did the heavy digging in the garden. He charged high for that, but he did it well, and Mrs Potter was thankful to get anybody. Mr Potter collected antique clocks. Dan inspected them, and studied the burglar alarm. He would need a vehicle for the clocks: Mr Potter's own Volvo Estate would do nicely. Mr Potter was a semi-retired insurance broker, spending three days a week in London; he had a lot of money but he spent little of it locally. His wife had been on the stage, people said; though pretty old she wore heavy purple lipstick. They were not gentry, to Dan's view, a fact which did not affect his attitude to them one way or the other. What did affect his attitude was that they were bloody-minded to the girls in the village shop. They thought having more money entitled them to overbearing arrogance. Also they grossly overpaid Dan in their garden, expecting to buy his devotion and buying his contempt.

Mrs Potter chatted to Dan while he hammered at the roof of an old cow-house. She was another one who liked his antique smock-frock performance. It made her feel wonderfully superior.

Dan asked innocent questions in his most treacly rural voice.

Of course Mrs Potter had heard about the Doctor's trout and Fred Mortimer's hay. She said she was very shocked, but Dan was not sure if this was true. He felt sure the Potters had not, themselves, had a letter from AgriSecurity.

A policeman crossed the rough grass towards the cow-house. He said the Super would be glad of a word with Dan; he was outside in the car.

Mrs Potter twittered; Dan assumed an expression of well-meaning stupidity. He followed the policeman out on to the road. The Superintendent was sitting in the back of a police car; Dan was told to join him there.

'Criminals,' said the Superintendent, 'often give themselves away by spending a lot of money.'

'Ay,' said Dan, thinking of the double gins in the Chestnut Horse.

'Or,' said the Superintendent, 'they need money. Sometimes a man needs a lot of money for a good reason. Treatment, let us say, for a sick child.'

'Child,' repeated Dan stupidly, disquieted by this line of talk.

'We spent some time today with Dr Smith, which will hardly surprise you. Like everybody else we have talked to, he has seen no signs of unexpected lavishness.'

'Eh?'

'Free spending. But as to people needing money, he was helpful. He remembers giving you the name of a Harley Street specialist, with regard to your mother's arthritic hip. I telephoned the specialist from Dr Smith's surgery. They read me your letter over the telephone. How do you expect to raise £1,200, Mallett?'

'A-bain't,' said Dan. 'A-b'lieved 'twould ben a tenner. A-give op the idea.'

'I can scarcely understand you when you mouth at me like that. You thought the operation would cost £10, with two artificial hip-joints and three weeks in a nursing-home. You have given up the idea, now that you know what it costs?'

'Ay.'

'Then why did you write to the specialist, asking for an appointment at the end of September?'

'Politeness, like.'

'I don't think you're the brain behind this. I think you're a tool, an underling. I think you're being paid by someone who's running a very dirty racket. I don't think you've written letters, but I think you've delivered them. I think you've made telephone calls. I think you set fire t , Mr Mortimer's hay, and put strychnine in Dr Smith's fishponds. If you didn't do it, you know who did do it. I want the name. Why not help us?'

'A-wisht a-could,' said Dan.

'I haven't evidence for an arrest. You're a clever little bastard. But I shall have. I'm watching you.'

The Superintendent's face seemed to Dan to have grown sharper and foxier, his eyes brighter and colder, since the calm morning by the stewponds. He looked worried, overworked and angry.

'The *only* way you can help yourself,' said the Superintendent, 'is to help us.'

'I wish I could, sir,' said Dan, sincerity making him speak, involuntarily, in a normal voice.

'Go away, you horrible little villain,' said the Superintendent. 'I'll see you again behind bars, probably tomorrow or the next day.'

7

Dan bicycled to the Calloways' with a new sense of urgency.

He was bound to be suspected of being mixed up in Agri-Security. If he'd been the Superintendent, he'd have suspected himself. His whole way of life made him a natural suspect for anything sly, secret, weird that went on in the countryside in the hours of darkness.

And they knew he needed £1,200.

And he *did* need £1,200. What they were doing, Agri-Security and the police between them, was making it impossible for him to get it.

They were threatening to make his whole life impossible. Was he going to be suspected of firing a barn every time he went out at night with a snare in his pocket?

Something had to be done, and the quicker the better.

The Calloways were having drinks on the lawn, the old couple and Camilla and some neighbours. Camilla was wearing her nice tight jeans with a cotton shirt of red and white checks.

Dan crossed the lawn towards them, grinning bashfully, torturing his cap in his hands. Camilla saw him first. She crimsoned and dropped her glass.

'My *dear* Camilla,' said her father-in-law, 'with gin the price it is . . .'

He turned and saw Dan and greeted him heartily. Everyone of his sort greeted Dan heartily – they thought they were being Old English squires. He did not seem to be overwhelmed with grief at the loss of his gun and silver.

Dan said, his voice low and slow and his accent ludicrously broad, 'A-cam fer ol' Cherry.'

'Does Miss Hadfield want her back?' asked Camilla. She was still very pink and her hand shook.

'Nay! 'Tes they windgalls d'want a-looken at.'

'Oh,' said Camilla, pretending to know what he was talking about. 'I'll come with you.'

'Oh you bastard,' she said, as soon as they were round the corner of the house.

Dan gave her his most disarming and lecherous grin. She laughed outright.

She said, 'Edwin's claiming for about six times what you pinched. Stuff they sold years ago, but it's still on the All-Risks policy. He's an awful old crook, really, even worse than you.'

He kissed her in the pony's shed. Cherry was pleased to see Dan, so that he was caught between two soft, adoring females. Cherry nuzzled at his behind, hoping for sugar, while Camilla occupied his front. The situation was affectionate but confusing.

Dan got down to the real reason for his visit: he asked Camilla about AgriSecurity's telephone call, and whether Mr Calloway had gone to the police. He had not. He had drawn £300 in mixed used notes from the bank, and he was going to do exactly what he was told. He knew about Fred Mortimer's barn and the Doctor's trout. He was playing safe. He was not showing public spirit. He was a sensible, selfish coward.

AgriSecurity had not yet telephoned, but it was obvious that they would do so any minute. Camilla promised to let Dan know when they did, and what was arranged about the payoff.

'But why are you involved, darling?' she asked.

Dan's reasons for being involved were clear and pressing. But he said, 'I don't know, truly. All those dead fish. It's gone on long enough. It's time to stop it. That's all about it, really.'

The telephone rang. They could just hear it in the shed. It stopped ringing. Someone had answered it. Dan and Camilla looked at each other. It might be anything, but it might be AgriSecurity.

Dan stayed in Cherry's shed while Camilla went away to find out. He pondered, pulling Cherry's ears.

What would the police be trying to do? They'd try to guess, just from the shape of the thing, who was behind it. A known criminal who'd been seen about; perhaps somebody who'd run a protection racket before. Criminals were supposed to sign their crimes. Was there a signature to poisoning rainbows in a stew-pond? The operation showed detailed local knowledge. Did that prove the boss was local? Not really – he could buy the knowledge he needed with a few drinks in the Chestnut Horse. Maybe the police could run everything they knew through a computer; maybe they'd come up with a prime suspect; Dan doubted it.

In practical terms, they could watch a place that had been threatened. But night after night? The whole of a big property, say like Fred Mortimer's? They could try again with the blood-hounds, with more cars and more men and more dogs. They could watch for the numbered notes turning up. They could try to trace AgriSecurity's typewriter. They could try to trace the telephone calls.

If Dan saw this much, so did AgriSecurity. If they thought a place was being watched, they'd go somewhere else. They'd sit on the notes they were given, mix them with others, change them somewhere busy. The typewriter they'd keep well hidden. Easy. Inside a sack of oats, or in a waterproof bag in a rabbit hole. The telephone calls? Dan imagined it was difficult to trace a call made through an automatic exchange. No doubt it could be done, if a lot of engineers were sitting ready at the exchange. The victim would be told to keep AgriSecurity talking; the engineers would zero in on the caller's telephone; a police car would rush there. The enemy would be aware of that. They'd keep the call short, just give instructions and ring off; and then get away from the telephone quick.

The best chance was the moment of payoff. It must be. The police must realize that and AgriSecurity must realize it.

Dan wanted to be there.

Camilla came back, pink and breathless. AgriSecurity had telephoned. Edwin had not recognized the voice. It was a man, with a slight local accent. The man had given orders, and Edwin was going to obey them.

The arrangements were very simple. AgriSecurity was not taking any elaborate precautions. It didn't have to. The trout floating belly-up in the Doctor's stewponds showed what happened when a trap was set.

Dan went out through the kitchen garden, so as not to disturb the gracious little party on the lawn. He looked into the enormous new greenhouse Mr Calloway had built. It had its own oil-fired, thermostatically controlled central heating, automatic watering, and automatically controlled ventilation. Most of it was given over to exotic flowers, which intrigued Dan with their fleshy, unfamiliar foliage and startling blossoms. Mr Calloway had planted grapevines, too. In a year or two there would be huge branches of muscatels and black grapes, and a special variety of pink ones. Dan looked forward to the grapes. He thought they would be good for his mother, what with vitamins and iron.

Dan bicycled home by way of Dave Sims's farm. He was interested to see that Dave had begun his harvest. The combine was circling a field of oats. Dave's wife would bake oatmeal bread, with some of the first grains they cut, and have a Lammastide loaf for the first of August. Loaf-mass it used to be, and slid itself into Lammas because people talked in a lazy way. She was a great one for traditions, Maggie Sims. Dan rather liked that. But he was glad he did not have to eat any of her oatmeal bread, which would be as hard and dry as a brick.

Nobody had damaged Dave's oats, or his combine. Dan wondered how much Dave had paid, to keep them safe.

They had named a time for Mr Calloway's payment, soon after the moon set. It was the time Dan himself would have chosen. It was another fine night, with a few clouds drifting across the moon in a light north-east wind.

The place seemed an odd choice, but really it was a good one. The money was to be placed on something which would be left in the middle of the village cricket-pitch. Mr Calloway, or his representative, was to park in the lane by the churchyard, go into the recreation ground, cross the recreation ground to the cricket-pitch, and leave the packet of notes right in the middle, on the close-mown wicket itself, on whatever he found there. He was to go straight back to his car, going nowhere near the wooden cricket pavilion or the new brick Memorial Hall. If there was any sign of police or anybody else: if the collector was interfered with in any way before getting to a telephone to report: if the money left on the wicket was not correct: then Mr Calloway would suffer as the Doctor had done.

That last bit of the orders was the most important part: it was AgriSecurity's insurance. At the same time the place made things easy for their agent. Dan thought the agent would get there well before the time of the drop, and hide somewhere at the edge of the cricket-field.

Who would he be, what sort of man? A violent professional criminal? If the police were there and got a look at him, one of them would know him. Or the police somewhere else would. Then they'd do what they called throw the book at him. (Dan pictured the literal hurling of a heavy legal volume, at the prisoner's head or his guts, across a small windowless room in a police station.) He'd talk to save himself, maybe, as Dan had been invited to. That must be as obvious to the boss of Agri-Security as all Dan's other bright ideas. Dan wondered again: how did the boss keep his soldiers under control?

Dan tucked his mother up early. He loped to the village, on foot, by moonlight. No one saw him. The pubs were still open;

a few people were about; Dan avoided them. He went past the Post Office to the church, and to the recreation ground which was opposite the church. Nobody saw him get there. He slipped over the wall into the Vicarage garden. Lights were still on in the Vicarage, but the windows were curtained. He crossed the garden to the tall privet hedge which bordered the recreation ground. The vicar's roses, in the night air, smelled almost intolerably sweet. Dan used the cover of the privet hedge to get down to the corner of the cricket-field. Then he climbed into Admiral Jenkyn's paddock. He used the cover of the rougher hedge which divided the paddock from the cricket-field. He made no sound and no one saw him.

When he reached the back of the cricket pavilion he prised out, with the blade of his knife, two loose boards he knew of. (The prosperous Vice-Presidents of the cricket club – people like the Admiral and Sir George Simpson – gave boozy parties for the players in the pavilion; Dan had often got away with half-full bottles of Scotch, and once with three full bottles.) The result looked an impossibly narrow gap for a grown man, but it was just big enough for Dan to squeeze through. He used his pencil flash inside the pavilion, and found a deckchair. He opened one of the windows beside the locked pavilion door, lifted the deckchair through, and followed it. He unfolded the chair on the pavilion's verandah. He had decided to wait in comfort. He was in the deep shadow cast by the roof of the verandah; he was invisible from a few feet away.

He settled, sighing, into the deckchair. Even in this relaxed position he was well above the level of the ground; the whole cricket-pitch was visible to him, the whole of the fence and hedge round it, the whole of the recreation ground between the cricket-pitch and the lane. His stick with the weighted knob was on the creosoted planks beside his chair. His knife was in his pocket. In his lap lay a pair of big German naval night-glasses. Admiral Jenkyn had looted them during the war; they were his only by right of armed theft from a defeated enemy.

Dan raised the glasses and scrutinized every yard of the

cricket-field's edge. He expected to see nothing and saw nothing. He turned the glasses on to the middle of the pitch, the shaven furlong of the wicket. There was something lying on the grass, almost exactly in the middle. It was invisible to the naked eye, and would have been invisible with ordinary binoculars. It was hardly visible through the big rubber-covered night-glasses. It was flat, about two foot square; it might be a piece of cloth, cardboard, plywood or dull metal. That was where the money was to go. Dan wondered why. To show Mr Calloway exactly where to deposit the packet? That was ridiculous. Why should it matter, within a few feet or yards, where he paid his blackmail?

Dan put it out of his mind, lowered the glasses to his lap, and sat waiting.

Like a heron, Dan could wait in absolute immobility for as long as he needed to. He stopped thinking about what was going on, about AgriSecurity and the police and his own involvement, because there was no more thinking he could usefully do. What he needed now was more knowledge; then he could do more thinking. He sat, his mind empty, his senses totally alert, as the shadows of the poplars cast by the full moon lengthened across the cricket-field. At last the field was all shadow as the moon sank below the woods beyond the church. Traffic ceased. Lights went out. Much of the world was asleep under the stars, though much was awake and busy. The tawny owls were noisy, after their silence, among the yews in the churchyard. The woodcocks would be feeding on the marshy ground beyond the river woods, heads cocked on one side and long bills probing the mud. Vixens would be coming out of their earths, with families of full-grown cubs, to catch rabbits and ground-roosting birds and moles and free-range hens. Dan, waiting motionless like a night heron, was one with these creatures.

Someone started a small motor-scooter in the lane by the churchyard. He revved the engine, roaring it, repeatedly, on and on. It sounded like a power saw. The noise was shocking in the quiet night. Presumably he thought there was something wrong with the engine; but it sounded all right. It was as though, even at this time of night at the edge of a sleeping village, he was making a lot of noise for the sake of it.

Dan realized that that was exactly what he was doing. He was covering, with the shattering noise of his little two-stroke, the much smaller noises being made by a friend. The friend was creeping into position somewhere at the edge of the cricket-field. They were taking this precaution just in case someone was watching and listening for them. They were very careful people.

Dan searched the edge of the cricket-field again with the night-glasses. The hedges showed up clearly in the starlight, but it was very black under them. He had very little hope of seeing anything, especially as they were taking so much trouble.

After a long time the motor-bike's engine changed tone as the rider clicked into gear. He rode off towards the middle of the village. Probably his face was covered with a scarf, and his number-plates caked with deliberate mud. He was away. He had done his bit. What he had done was completely innocent and totally effective. A platoon of men could have burrowed into the hedge, anywhere at the edge of the field, without Dan hearing anything over the noise of the motor-scooter.

It could now be assumed there were two of them watching the wicket in the middle of the cricket-field.

Some time later a car purred slowly down Church Lane with dipped headlights. It stopped and the engine cut. The driver left his sidelights on. The car door opened and closed. Faint, but quite clear in the still night, Dan heard the click of the catch on the gate into the recreation ground.

He raised the night-glasses, and focused on a tall figure walking between the swings and seesaws of the recreation ground. Mr Calloway had not trusted anybody else. He did exactly what he had been told to do. He walked without hesitation directly to the wicket, bent, put something that looked like a large book on the square object in the middle of the wicket.

He walked briskly back the way he had come. He looked about him as he walked, but he did not pause or deviate from a straight line. He was very anxious not to have his property damaged.

The gate clicked. The car door clicked. The engine coughed to life and the headlights came on. The car whispered to the next corner, stopped, reversed, turned. For a moment the lights swept across the recreation ground and the cricket-field; for a moment the packet in the middle of the wicket showed up like a pimple on a buttock. Then the car passed the church again and accelerated away. Mr Calloway was off. Like the motor-cyclist, he had done his bit.

Dan sat waiting, alert and motionless as a heron, eyes and ears straining for the slightest indication of movement. Nothing moved. There was no sound except the wild lament of the owls in the churchyard.

For the third time, Dan inspected every yard of the edge of the cricket-pitch with the night-glasses. He saw nothing. If a man was anywhere there he was well hidden. If he was moving his movements were small and cautious.

Dan turned the glasses on to the package on its square of stuff in the middle of the wicket.

His heart lurched. It was not there.

8

Dan was dumbfounded, incredulous. There was no way the money could have been picked up, moved, without his seeing. Had he gone into a coma for two minutes? Had a trained bird swooped down out of the night sky and grabbed it? Had it vaporized? Were his own eyes working properly? He blinked them. He looked at other things. His eyes were fine.

He began to search with the glasses the slightly longer grass near the wicket. Then he saw the book-like package on the square of whatever it was. It had moved twenty yards. Dan blinked again, doubting not his eyes but his sanity.

It began to move on, by magic or magnetism, gently across the grass. It moved not at a steady rate but in jerks, stopping for a second at a time and then sliding on. It looked alive. It was moving in an exact straight line, towards a point in the hedge about thirty yards from Dan, between him and the lane, near the end of the Vicarage privet hedge. Dan thought he could just hear the very faint whispering noise of the thing sliding over the dry grass.

He got it. It was being pulled to the hedge on a string. The square of stuff on the wicket had been planted there as soon as it got dark, one end of a long piece of string attached to it. The string had been led across the grass to the hedge, to a point which a man could reach secretly and leave quickly. Probably the string was green garden twine, or dyed deep-sea fishing line, invisible on the grass. Mr Calloway's orders insured that he wouldn't trip on it or foul it up.

Dan felt reluctant admiration. It was a better scheme than he'd thought of for them. They were clever, really clever, as well

as careful and bloody-minded and vicious. That was all he had
added to his knowledge, all he was going to learn from tonight
if he stayed where he was on the verandah. In a couple of minutes the package of money and the square of stuff would dis-
appear into the hedge. Then the man was mobile. He probably
had a bicycle hidden just inside the churchyard, leaning up
against the low wall on the other side. Dan had no chance of
catching him once he got to his bicycle, and very little of seeing
his face.

But until the package reached the hedge, the man was tied
where he was, tied to the end of his string. To learn any more,
to do any good tonight, Dan must get to him before the package
got to him. To do what? Collar him and make him talk.

Could he? The police had plenty of various methods unavailable to Dan, owing to having cars and radios and gaols, and
armies of men, and the law behind them. But Dan had a few
methods unavailable to the police. They might make a man talk
by throwing the book at him; he might make a man talk by
throwing other things.

He might also, while he was at it, get the money.

The man in the hedge would be mighty confident at this
moment. Already he'd feel the package in his hands, and his
arse on the saddle of his bicycle. He would not be relaxed, but
he'd be focusing on the string and the package. He'd be licking
his lips.

Dan put the night-glasses gently down on the boards beside
his chair. He got up carefully out of the chair. It creaked, but
very softly. Standing up, Dan could just see, without the night-
glasses, the package crawling across the grass; it stopped for
several seconds, then gave a small lurch and slid on. Dan
imagined the man pausing to coil his string or clear a tangle.

What Dan wanted now was a spinning-rod, and a lead plug
armed with a big treble. He could have tossed the plug behind
the string, caught the string in the hooks, pulled it towards
himself. There was no other way he could catch the string or
the package without showing himself. He thought of, but imme-

diately rejected, trying to use a cricket stump as a javelin: or trying to throw a cricket bag far enough to land on top of the string.

The best thing would have been to climb out of the back of the pavilion, creep to where the man was, and collar him while he was concentrating on his string. But it was impossible to go quietly enough. Dan thought that if anyone could do it, he could; but even he couldn't. It meant going through the Admiral's hedge. It was a thick mixed hedge, thorn, ash, oak, holly, snowberry, brambles, briar roses, with festoons of honeysuckle and briony and bindweed. A grass-snake couldn't go through it quietly enough.

So the plan was to run out, grab the package, run on: and get the man out of the hedge and chasing him. They could play catch-as-catch-can all night in the recreation ground, or among the graves in the churchyard. Dan would surely get a look at the man, even in the dark, and find out something about him. But he expected to do better than that. He didn't think the man would run away without the money, anyway not before dawn. If they got into the churchyard, Dan thought he'd get a chance to kick in the spokes of the bicycle wheels, if the man had a bicycle and if it was in the churchyard.

The package was twenty-five yards from the pavilion verandah, and the same distance from the Vicarage hedge. It stopped, started again. Dan would pick it up at a run, and be pretty well clear of the cricket-pitch before the man had got himself out of the hedge.

Now. Dan pulled his cap down firmly on his head, and took a good grip of his weighted stick. He jumped down the steps of the verandah and hared across the grass to the package. He hardly slowed as he bent to pick the package from the ground. The thing it sat on, the little sledge, was a square of stiffened canvas. The string was almost invisible. The package was a supermarket carrier-bag.

Dan sped towards the recreation ground. He did not look round – there'd be time enough for that. He had a long flying start over the man in the hedge. He could easily get clear away with the money. He was safe. The man couldn't have seen his face in the dark. It was tempting. But Dan wanted to see the man's face, hear him talk. He'd get away with the money afterwards.

Dan raced to the edge of the cricket-pitch. He hurdled the low fence into the recreation ground. It was very dark. He stopped and turned, a hand on one of the high metal frames of the children's swings. He could just see that the man had come out of the hedge. He was a small man, Dan's size, which was highly encouraging. He was in no hurry. He trotted after Dan, making no apparent effort to catch him. Dan imagined he was scared. Dan decided to let him get a lot nearer, then to nip into the churchyard.

Dan was panting, but he grinned to himself. Things were working out nicely. It depended on how much the man knew, and how much he would tell of what he knew. Dan thought he would tell everything he knew, since he was a small man, advancing tentatively across the grass, seeming nervous. Dan expected, by one means or another, to get the name of the boss of AgriSecurity. Probably Dan would give the man to the police, with the boss's name. He would then have to decide what to do with Mr Calloway's money.

Apart from Dan's breathing, there was no sound except the scream of an owl. The light north-east wind had dropped; it was a dead-quiet night. The man advancing nervously across the cricket-field made no noise on the grass.

Dan waited, just inside the frame of the children's swings. He heard, from above, a tiny screech of metal on metal. It was a minute noise, no louder than the buzz of a sleepy insect. But it was not the noise of any insect. The swings were solid oak planks hanging from the bar by big chains; they were massive, safe, indestructible swings, given to the village after the war. The noise Dan heard was the ring at the top of the chain, moving on the bar. The swing was moving. But there was no wind. Someone was moving it.

Dan threw himself full length on the ground as the heavy swing whistled over him. It would have caught him on the base of the skull, certainly knocking him cold, possibly killing him.

The realization flashed into his head: the man in the hedge had a friend. He'd expected only one but there were two. And they were playing rough.

Dan rolled over half a dozen times in case the friend dived, then jumped into a crouch and turned, gripping his stick.

The man was big – over six foot, broad, seeming neckless in the dark, seeming to have a monstrous round head. Starlight gleamed on the oversized shiny skull. His face seemed to be black. He was wearing a crash-helmet, and he had a scarf over his face. He was the man with the motor-scooter. He had stopped, doubled back, waited in hiding. It was an additional precaution and a very good one.

The big man did not make a dive for Dan, which he expected and was ready for, but circled round him. He moved lightly and fast, like a dancer. He was getting between Dan and escape, and the other man was trotting up from the cricket-field. Dan was between them, with their money.

Dan cursed himself. Another man, a cover, a sentry, was such an obvious precaution for these people to take. He ought to have guessed they'd take it. But he'd run on like a fool, full of stupid self-confidence, patting himself on the back; and now he was in it up to his neck, caught between the two of them, and one of the two twice his weight without being fat or slow. And the big man was wearing a crash-helmet: Dan's loaded stick would bounce off his head without him feeling it.

Of course the stick might do some damage to a different part of the big man. It might damage the man from the hedge. What was useless as a weapon was the plastic bag. Dan tucked it down the front of his shirt. That gave him a free hand for his knife or anything else.

Dan kept his eyes flickering left and right, trying to keep tabs on both men. The big man was making no effort to attack: he was waiting for his friend. The smaller one trotted un-

79

hurriedly to the edge of the cricket-field, and scrambled over the fence. He stopped five yards from Dan. Dan was five yards from the big man.

Dan's only way out of this was on to the lane or on to the cricket-field. The third side of the recreation ground was bounded by the Vicarage hedge, which had chestnut palings behind it to keep dogs out of the garden. Dan could get through it, but not quickly. The fourth side had the high stop-netting of two derelict tennis-courts. Dan could climb it, but not quickly. It was no good making a dash either of those ways. He had to get past the big man or the small man. Obviously it had to be the small man.

The small man had a pistol in his hand. Dan had not expected that.

The small man said, 'The game's over. Let's have it.'

Dan didn't recognize the voice. It was nobody he knew. It was a local voice. The face, at five yards' distance, was no more than a pale blur in the starlight.

Would he use the gun? Why not? People would hear the bang. Some would ignore it. Bangs were common – bird-scarers, people shooting pigeons and rooks and jays and rabbits and squirrels – but not at this time of night. A bang would bring people out to look. They'd find Dan, but not the two men or the money.

Dan backed a few paces so that he could see both men. They came with him, cutting off his escape.

The smaller man said, 'No more of the old-time dancin', eh? Just pull it out and drop it on the ground and nobody won't get hurt.'

'Get on, do,' said the big man. He had an unexpectedly high voice, almost womanish. He sounded impatient. He wanted to get home to bed: or perhaps they had another job tonight.

Dan thought the small man would use the gun, but only as a last resort. He'd be reluctant to make a loud bang in the middle of a quiet night. Possibly he'd be reluctant to do a murder. In that hope, Dan backed a further few feet. But at the same time, to show willing, he thrust his hand down the front of his shirt and started tugging the package out.

The men came with him. The big one was blocking the way to the lane and churchyard, the smaller one and his pistol the way to the cricket-field.

Dan backed, as he knew he would, up against the children's seesaw. It was a massive oak plank, fifteen foot long by a foot wide, with a kind of wooden saddle at each end. A young child could sit in the saddle and grasp a wooden pommel in front of him. The fulcrum was a heavy pyramid of tubular iron. The plank swivelled on it, so the seesaw could go round and round as well as up and down. It was popular with the village children; it was popular with Dan, too.

He pulled Mr Calloway's plastic bag out of the front of his shirt, and put it on the seesaw by the fulcrum. Then he backed to the end of the plank. He lifted his end so that the other sloped down towards the grass. The plastic bag slid along the sloping plank, and fell off on to the grass near its end. Dan let his hand rest idly on his end of the seesaw.

'Okay,' said Dan. He imitated the big man's high voice, completely disguising his own.

'Sensible lad,' said the smaller man.

He bent down to pick up the package.

With all his strength, Dan heaved his end of the seesaw sideways, across the front of his body, chest high. The other end swung in a violent arc six inches above the ground. The heavy oak plank smashed into the small man as he was picking up the package. It hit him on the wrist and on the shins. He squealed like a rabbit and dropped the package and his gun. Dan dived forward and picked up the gun. He still had his stick in his other hand, holding it by the ferrule. He kicked the package of money clear, at the same time swinging the knob of his stick against the man's head. It hit with a solid clunk. The man buckled and went down untidily. He whimpered. He was not knocked out but he was hurt and frightened.

The big man took a step forward, then stopped uncertainly.

Dan was pointing the gun at him. Dan had never before in his life held a pistol, but he knew how it was done.

He snarled, in his unfamiliar high voice, 'All right, friend, start talking.'

'Eh?' said the big man.

'Who's your boss?'

'I dunno.'

'Try harder.'

'Honest! I dunno!'

'Try harder, sweetheart, or I'll plug you in the guts.'

After all the gangster movies he'd seen, the words came easily to Dan. But shooting the man in the belly would not have come easily. He considered shooting him in the leg, if he could hit it in the dark.

'Honest!' wailed the big man again. 'We gets a message on the phone. We don't know no name, nothin'.'

The man was powerful and agile, but he was frightened of the gun in Dan's hand. Probably no one had ever pointed a gun at him before. Dan was sure he was a villain, a small-time thug. Perhaps he'd pointed guns at other people, in sub-Post Offices and all-night filling stations, but he'd never been on the receiving end. He was as new to this scene as Dan was. But he still said he knew nothing.

'Yeah?' snarled Dan, gesturing with the gun as he had seen hoodlums do it on television. 'How were you getting the money to him, then?'

'We leaves it where he says.'

'Where?'

'I dunno. He'll tell us on the phone.'

'How did you get to work for him, if you never met him?'

'It were done on the phone.'

'How does he pay you?'

'He leaves it where he says. We pick it up.'

'Where do you come from?'

'Milchester way. Been sleepin' rough.'

'With a telephone?'

'We uses the box in the Post Office.

'And with a motor-bike?'

'That's borrowed, like.'

Dan could get nothing more out of the big man, frightened as the man was of the gun. He knew nothing about his boss except a voice on the telephone. He recognized the voice when he heard it, but he didn't know whose voice it was.

Dan ordered the big man to kneel on the ground beside his friend. He could thus cover them both with the gun. The smaller man was sitting up, whimpering, nursing his wrist. He said Dan had broken it.

'Good,' said Dan, busy with his thoughts.

The small man exactly echoed his friend. He had been called to the telephone in a Milchester pub. A strange voice offered him a job. He needed the work, he needed the money, he was skint. He did not know the boss's name or where he lived. The approach always came from the boss.

'But you phone him?'

'Never.'

'You must have.'

'Never. Dunno the number – dunno who to ask for.'

The small man was frightened of the gun, too. He was whimpering with the pain of his wrist. He was frightened of the heavy stick which Dan was still holding by the ferrule in his left hand. But he persisted that he knew no more. Short of torture, Dan could get no more out of him. Maybe there was no more to get.

Dan picked up the packet of money and stowed it away again in the front of his shirt. He backed to the gate on to the lane, waving the gun. The big man was trying to help his friend. The small man screamed when the big man tried to look at his wrist.

The motor-scooter was in full view, leaning against the churchyard wall. Dan opened the tap for the gas, twisted the throttle, and kicked the little engine to life. He switched on the lights, straddled the machine, and gunned away down the lane. He had never passed a test or held a licence, but he had ridden dozens of motor-bikes. He was not impressed with this one, but he was glad of it. He was very tired.

As he burbled through the village he remembered the Admiral's night-glasses, the deckchair, the missing planks in the back of the pavilion. It showed how tired he was, that he could have forgotten all that; it showed how scared he'd been, for a short time, there in the recreation ground. It was a pity about the planks. New ones would be put in, too firmly to be removed except with heavy tools and a lot of noise. It was annoying about the glasses, too, which were sometimes very useful. Maybe he could recover them from the Admiral's house, some night, not too soon. Meanwhile they were covered with Dan's fingerprints, which probably didn't matter at all.

Dan crossed the bridge over the river, and headed for home.

The big man must have lied. He must know *something* about the boss. They both must. More than they told Dan. Yet they were scared. He had scared them with the gun, and he'd scared the little one with the stick. But they still told him nothing, absolutely nothing. They were very brave and very loyal.

No they weren't. They were more scared of the boss than they were of Dan's gun. Perhaps he had something on them. Enough to stop them squeezing him for more money, enough to keep their mouths shut even at the point of a gun. He must have frightened them badly. He must be a frightening man.

What were they doing now, those two? Telephoning their boss from the coin-box outside the Post Office, reporting that they'd got the money and lost it. Telephoning how? Not waiting for a call to the box – that was impossible, the timing couldn't be that accurately fixed in advance. They must be telephoning him. They *must* have a number.

Dan cursed himself, and cursed the fatigue that had dulled his brain. Of course they must have a number. The man in Yewstop Lane must have had a number.

Dan slowed to a crawl, swung the scooter round in a U-turn,

and rode as fast as the little machine would go all the way back to the village, over the bridge, to the Post Office.

The bland light shone in the telephone box. The box was empty. The street was empty. They had rung the number they knew, and gone where they were told to.

Where? The Calloways'. Reprisals. A punishment, for grabbing his money back after he'd paid it. Nothing could be more certain. It was another thing Dan should have thought of, long ago, if he hadn't been so tired.

He went on through the village. He stopped the scooter, switched off, and hid it in a clump of bracken. He went very carefully, looking and listening, stalking up towards the house.

AgriSecurity would have to assume Mr Calloway had planted him there in the pavilion. Nobody else, as far as they knew, knew about the arrangement. AgriSecurity had to assume Mr Calloway had disobeyed orders. He'd be hit for sure. It was rather bad luck on him, perhaps. The telephone box outside the Post Office was a two-minute walk from the recreation ground. It was three-quarters of an hour since Dan had left the recreation ground. It was forty-three minutes, then, since the two had reported to their boss. AgriSecurity moved fast when it was angry. The Doctor's trout were poisoned pretty soon after the business in Yewstop Lane. They could have a man or an army at the Calloways' by now. Would Mr Calloway be expecting them, mounting any sort of sentry? No, of course not, he thought he was safe, he'd bought protection.

Dan felt for the gun in his pocket. It wasn't there. He'd dropped it, perhaps when he was pushing the motor-scooter into the bracken. Pity. It was reassuring.

Dan slipped through the gate into the orchard. He prowled, with extreme caution, between the young trees towards the kitchen garden.

Then he heard the explosion.

9

There was glass all over the kitchen garden. The enormous greenhouse was a twisted skeleton. The precious exotic flowers were wide-strewn shreds of compost.

'Gelignite,' murmured Dan, awed by the extent of the mess. He knew nothing about explosives, but the news had made the name familiar. It was what they used in quarries and for making motorways; it was what terrorists got hold of.

No grapes for the old lady. This thing was getting really annoying.

Dan blamed himself, to a small extent, for the explosion. Mr Calloway had paid, but the payment nestled against Dan's ribs. It was hard on Mr Calloway.

But it was in the public interest. Dan had found a few things out, at the cost of Mr Calloway's greenhouse. AgriSecurity had contact, or could easily make contact, with the local criminal element. It knew who the bad men were and how to get hold of them. It had this knowledge, as well as local knowledge of farms and gardens and fishponds. It had a telephone, and its men had the telephone number. Dan cursed himself for failing to get the number.

Dan heard shouts and running feet. He turned and ran himself, ran like hell across the orchard and across the fields. To be seen at the house, at a moment like this, would be very embarrassing. To be collared with the money under his shirt – that would be a ten-year sentence.

He fetched up, panting, in the lane by Cobb Wood. There was nobody about. Dan found he was even more tired than he'd thought. He wanted to ride the motor-scooter home. He decided against it. The machine committed him to the roads, and there'd be police cars on the roads after the explosion. The scooter was all right where it was. Probably nobody would find it until the bracken died down in the winter, unless a young couple bunked up in there. (Bracken was perfect for that, as Dan knew from long experience: it grew tall and thick, no nettles or thistles grew under it, and it kept the flies away; once girls got used to it they liked it, unless they were frightened of snakes or spiders.) Even if the scooter was found, it didn't greatly matter. Nobody knew Dan had ridden it. The big man had stolen it.

The sky was beginning to pale when Dan got home, more exhausted than he ever remembered feeling. He hid the money in the undergrowth well away from the cottage; it would be safe in the plastic bag. He greeted the dogs and quieted their excited clamour. His mother called to him fretfully as he opened the cottage door. She said the dogs had just woken her up, but he guessed she'd been awake for a long time, in pain, waiting for him, worrying.

The police were calling to see everybody in the neighbourhood, over a wide area. Not *everybody* – not down-and-outs like Dan and his mother – but all substantial farmers, landowners, householders, principal tradesmen, owners of sporting rights: people who had something of value to protect and money to pay for its protection. The police were as inconspicuous as they could be, but it was noticed and talked about, as everything is in the country.

Dan knew about it as soon as anybody, because he went about the countryside on various jobs, and talked to all sorts of people, and kept his eyes and ears open.

The police were trying to find every single person who'd had a letter from AgriSecurity; they were trying to look at all the letters. Some people had paid and kept quiet; the police wanted to know how they'd paid, who they'd seen, what voices they'd heard.

An awful lot of policemen were about – far more than Dan liked to see – both uniformed and detectives. Several asked the way to well-known local places. Obviously they came from different parts of the County. Dan heard it said that the Chief Constable was deploying every man he could.

The gossip in the Chestnut Horse was that they weren't getting very far, because people were scared to help them. Dan guessed there were plenty of people who'd paid, and were still paying, and would go on paying, because of the Doctor's trout, Fred Mortimer's barn, Mr Calloway's greenhouse. He heard that Admiral Jenkyn was seen going out late at night, which wasn't like him. When he had a job at the Jenkyns', patching the side of the tool-shed, he asked Mrs Jenkyn about it. He was at his most simple and innocent, a child of nature, practically a pixie. Everybody told him everything when he put that face on: but Mrs Jenkyn wouldn't tell him anything, which wasn't like her. Dan thought she was frightened to talk about it.

Dan went to see Camilla.

A man from the insurance company, as well as the police, had come about the burglary and the greenhouse. Edwin had lied like a trooper, Camilla said, about what silver was missing. There wouldn't be any trouble about the money. Camilla said she was shocked by this. Dan saw that it was true. She was not out of the same herd as the old people. She had a basic honesty, as well as guts, which made her a member of a different species.

Mr Calloway had had another letter from AgriSecurity, very angry indeed. It accused him of stealing the money back after he'd paid it. That was why his greenhouse had been blown up, as a punishment for his dishonesty and as a warning. There was plenty more explosive where that came from, the letter said. Now Mr Calloway was to get £500 in old notes. He was given a few days to get the money. Then he'd be told where to take it.

The harvest began in earnest, all over the district, the barley and oats first, and then the red-gold oceans of wheat. The combines were starting early and finishing late. How much protection was being secretly paid to keep those combines on the job before the weather broke? To save the tons of grain-sacks from a bucket of petrol and a match?

Fred Mortimer had an army of combines in his cornfields. It was miraculous how quickly the land was cleared – changed from the billowing seas of grain into a desert of stubble.

One of Fred's fields was left uncut. Dan saw without surprise that it was the dirty barley. Fred must have decided that it wasn't worth harvesting. He'd burn, then spray when the weeds showed, then drill turnips without bothering to plough: an ugly way to farm. Fred was one of the ones who was helping the police. No doubt he could afford any damage AgriSecurity did, being properly insured. He'd had a second letter, everybody knew that, he talked about it in the pub. Whether he'd had the follow-up telephone call Dan didn't know. He thought it was time to find out.

Dan met young Harry Barnett in the village, lugubrious as usual, on his way to the Chestnut Horse. Harry knew Dan was interested in the letters people were getting. Everyone was interested. People with something to lose were terrified; people with nothing to lose were morbidly fascinated. Dan enquired about Fred Mortimer. Harry said he'd been in the pub yesterday supper-time, and Fred Mortimer's cowman had come in, old Curly Godden. Fred Mortimer was in a rare stew, Curly said, because the AgriSecurity people had phoned him at last. The money they wanted was terrible, a terrible sum, to protect Fred's property, all of it Fred went to the police. What they planned Curly Godden didn't know, but they planned something, Fred and the police. He was a sharp one, that Fred, and Harry Barnett didn't envy anyone who tried to muck him about. He hoped Fred and the police would come down like a ton of rubble on the bastards who had poisoned the trout.

Dan could keep track of Curly Godden's movements, that evening, simply by keeping a casual eye on Fred Mortimer's cattle. He was able to meet Curly, by the purest chance, as Curly bicycled home.

Curly had a dark red face and the corkscrew hair, now white, which accounted for what everybody had called him for fifty years. His manner was awesomely dignified, always had been. As a child Dan had thought him an important and frightening person; later Dan realized that Curly used his dignified manner and respectable appearance to cloak all kinds of activities. They were not often very serious. He confined his poaching to a few fish drag-lined out of the river, his theft to shoplifting in the Milchester supermarkets. Dan knew about it, as creatures of the same species recognize each other, but very few other people did. The few said that Curly's wife drove him to it. She had ideas above a cowman's wages. Luckily for Curly, her ideas did not extend beyond an occasional fresh trout and a few bars of scented pink soap.

The two bad characters said good evening to each other, with proper caution. Dan asked, ever so casually, about Fred Mortimer and the police, having (he said) heard something about it in the Chestnut Horse.

'And why,' asked Curly with freezing dignity, 'are you interested, Dan bloody Mallett?'

'I heard,' said Dan reflectively, 'they're goin' to use grenades and tommy-guns.'

'Gord. Where d'ye hear *that*?'

'In Milchester,' said Dan. 'In the Public Convenience. Two blokes was talking. I couldn't see 'em – they was havin' a slash on the other side o' the marbles.'

'Let 'em come,' said Curly. 'We're settin' with guns an'

pitchforks all over the farm. With I dunno how many coppers.'

'Night after night, Curly?'

'O'course. We'll get un. They'll be apprehended, some on 'em missin' a leg.'

So Fred Mortimer and the police had made the plan Dan had thought was impossible, the blanket guarding of a big farm when the farmer had refused to pay protection. The police must be bringing in a bloody battalion, and Fred probably had a lot of extra hands too.

One more wouldn't be noticed.

An idea was stirring in Dan's mind. He had a notion to watch where he thought not many people would be watching.

He sat out, most of the night, one night and two nights and three. Camilla, when he visited her, complained that he was sleepy.

He knew that he was not at his best: but it was vital to keep in touch with her. He had to know what was happening. Nothing was happening. The Calloways had not heard any more from AgriSecurity. It was more than ever obvious that Agri-Security was at full stretch, making threats and collecting money from farmers bringing in their harvest. The income, Dan thought, must be tremendous.

Dan did not intend to waste his nights on Fred Mortimer's farm. He took old Pansy and he carried a partridge net. The first three dawns it was no good, because there were other watchers in sight. They were not very near; they did not see him; but if he'd tried to use the dog and the net he would have been spotted.

On the fourth night the moon, a little past full, blazed white-gold out of a clear sky; she turned the country into a crossword-puzzle of dense black blots on a silvered background. Dan, deep in a ditch in one of the blackest shadows, saw no movement and heard no voices. He was certain Fred Mortimer's watchers had been pulled away to guard another part of the farm. It suited him fine; it was also what he'd expected.

Pansy was a real old-fashioned pointer, a complete down-charge dog. If Dan raised a hand with the palm down, Pansy would sink to the ground and freeze; she would stay motionless until he let her go by waving at her. It was quite safe to bring her out these nights: nothing she did would give Dan's presence away to a man going by a yard from their heads. Like Dan himself, she would be alert while she lay motionless, although unlike him she could sleep all day. She was pleased to be out with him although, faithful to the tradition of her breed, she was too dour to show it.

Dan's net was another piece of green nylon netting for strawberries and currant bushes. It was in the shape of a half-open fan, the outer edges spoked with eight-foot wands of bamboo. Holding the two bamboos with the net outstretched fanwise between them, he could cover quite an area of ground. It was useful that the netting was very light.

Dan also had with him, each night, his Zeiss binoculars and Sir George Simpson's flask, and (out of habit) his knife and his weighted blackthorn.

After the blazing moon, the fourth dawn had the look and smell, for the first time, of real autumn. Mist lay like a blanket on the low ground, with trees rising out of it as though they were rooted in the mist. There was a heavy dew; Dan and Pansy were both soaking when the sky began to pale. The spiders had been intensely busy in the moonlight and in the dark – every square yard of dew-soaked countryside was festooned with dozens of little silver cobwebs close to the ground. Dan felt sad to break them, after all the labour of the spinners.

As soon as it was light enough for Pansy to see, Dan waved her into the stubble. She was up out of their ditch like a snake, and began gently quartering the field. She went at it with none of the dash of a setter, but in a sly and methodical way, moving upwind, nose and eyes straining, belly close to the ground. Dan could barely see her, moving stealthily through the mist; had he not known she was there, he would never have noticed her.

She stopped moving. She stood as though carved, holding her point, her plumed tail flat behind her, her nose extended, one foreleg bent. She was telling Dan that on the ground a few yards in front of her a covey of partridges was feeding in the stubble.

Dan moved as unhurriedly and discreetly as his clever old dog. Using the cover of hedge and ditch and folds in the ground, keeping low, going delicately, he fetched a long compass until he came up behind the covey. Once upon a time a man would have come out with a hawk for this chase. Not a sparrowhawk or a goshawk, scudding over the ground and pouncing, but a real long-winged falcon, a glorious peregrine. The falcon would have spiralled high over the stubble, and then the partridges would have stuck to the ground as though glued. Or they had kites in the old days that looked like hawks. Fly one of those over a covey and it had the same effect, so people said. It was something Dan wanted to try, but there was no one he trusted enough to fly a kite-hawk while he netted a covey during the close season. As it was, he was relying on the hypnotic eye of a single old pointer to make the partridges stay put. It would work if he himself was stealthy enough.

He fetched up, at the end of his circuit, facing Pansy at thirty yards' distance, the covey between him and her. He guessed he was a bare furlong from the birds. He straightened very slowly from the cover of the hedge; he raised the binoculars, hanging on a thong round his neck; and searched the ground in front of Pansy. He saw three partridges, as flat to the ground as fried eggs, their stupid heads turned towards Pansy, their eyes held by hers; he guessed there were more, maybe ten or a dozen.

The sky was getting paler. There was nobody about. A few birds were whistling and chattering. There was no other sound. Beyond the stubble, Fred Mortimer's unharvested barley showed through the mist as white as a snowfall.

Dan began to creep, foot by stealthy foot, over the stubble towards Pansy. He had put down his stick and binoculars. He held a bamboo spoke in each hand; the net fanned in front of him, close to the ground, almost invisible.

He covered five yards, ten. He saw eight birds, tight to the ground, all fixed by Pansy's terrible eye. Pansy never by a flicker of a whisker showed she knew he was coming. She never moved her eyes from the birds; her tail stuck out behind her and her nose in front; her right foreleg was bent, the paw just clear of the ground; she held the point as though she'd been dipped in starch.

Dan inched forward another five yards, putting down his feet as though on valuable eggshells. He wanted another pointer, another man, a bigger net, a hawk in the sky, but he'd manage without. He saw how the covey was grouped on the ground, and planned where to whack down the net so as to catch the greatest number.

Another yard, and another. Dan stole forward in a crouch, his net ready, his concentration total, watching where he put his feet down, inching the net over the mesmerized partridges.

The birds heard it a split second before he did – *whoomp!* a strange muted noise like a gust of wind going down a tunnel. In spite of Pansy's hypnotic eye, the partridges catapulted off the ground like fat brown bullets. Dan slammed down the net, catching only three. The rest whirred away to his left, then swung round behind him. Pansy rushed forward, knowing that her job was done, and Dan scrambled to keep the captured birds in the net. As soon as he could, three seconds after the strange noise, he looked up to see what had happened.

Bright flames were walking like an army through Fred Mortimer's barley. The *whoomp* was explained. It was petrol. That got the fire going in spite of the heavy dew; now nothing in the world would stop it till it reached the headlands.

A man was running away. He was a long way off, barely visible in the dawn mist. Dan had no idea who he was. He was perfectly safe.

It was all working out as Dan expected. He knew what was happening now. He knew who was AgriSecurity.

But still nobody would believe him. The thing to do, then, was either to stop it, or prove what was happening so the police would stop it. It was not going to be easy to do either. But unless the thing was stopped, there was no end to destruction and extortion. There was no end to Dan's troubles.

Dan wrung the necks of his partridges – one adult, two young but full-grown – and slipped them into his poacher's pocket. He gave Pansy a lump of sugar, and began rolling up his net round the bamboo spokes. A muffled roar came from the barley, and a crackle that came and went over the roar. In the dark of the night the flames would have been seen from miles away; now in the brightening dawn they might not be seen at all. In clear air the smoke would have been seen from miles away; now in the heavy mist it might not be seen at all.

Neither fire nor smoke was seen. There was no sight or sound of a car on Yewstop Lane, no shouting through the mist, no whistle. The noise of the fire had already softened to a hiss, and the flames were scarcely visible in the brightening daylight. Dan decided to take a closer look. Of course the police would poke about, when they finally got here, but by that time any evidence might have been swept away. And something might mean something to Dan that wouldn't mean anything to the police. They were out of their depth here. Unlike Dan, they didn't know who AgriSecurity was. At the rate they were going, they never would.

Dan's instinct was to get far away quickly. But his brain said that any scrap of new evidence was worth looking for. He obeyed his brain instead of his instinct, and it very nearly killed him.

He collected his blackthorn and binoculars. With Pansy at heel, he loped across the stubble to the smoking, flickering, hissing, soot-black acres. The fire had stopped at a tractor-track down the edge of the stubble. It had not damaged the fence – Fred had put in metal fenceposts here. The edges of the headlands were charred as though painted with tar along the sides. A branch here and there was scorched, but no real damage had been done to the trees overhanging the headland. The thorn hedge was untouched. Smoke rose thinly from the whole burned area.

Dan went along the ditch beside the field, passing the place where he and Pansy had spent the night. In the next field, empty grazing, six feet from the hedge, two five-gallon drums lay blatantly on the grass. One was called paint-thinner, one creosote, but both had held petrol. They were very ordinary, no doubt untraceable. The man had arrived while Dan was working his way behind the covey. He hadn't seen Dan in the mist, because Dan was in cover, stalking the partridges. The man must have moved pretty quietly himself – the partridges hadn't budged, and Dan had heard nothing. Pansy had probably heard him, but she was holding her point and a bomb wouldn't have shifted her. The man had sloshed out the petrol, thrown a match to it, and bolted like a rabbit into the mist.

The mist was clearing. It was high time Dan got away home. Pansy, looking at him crossly, certainly thought so. Dan sighed. He knew it all now. But he didn't know what to do with his knowledge, not without getting himself killed or put in gaol.

'Have a look here, sir,' called a voice from the trees.

'Hell,' said a voice Dan recognized as the foxy Superintendent's.

Dan was already in his familiar ditch, Pansy's head under his head. She'd seen the flat of his hand; she'd stay put. But they were not well hidden, not by broad daylight. Pansy was black and white and blue-mottled – not bad camouflage, but the white was more or less white. Dan was carrying a monogrammed silver flask, expensive imported binoculars, and three partridges taken on private land out of season. And he was on the spot. The police only needed a bit more evidence against him. His being here was the evidence they needed.

He lay in the ditch, with Pansy, for four hours.

Sometimes three pairs of boots were standing a yard from his head. Sometimes a great silence fell. Then, keeping the flat of his hand on Pansy's head, Dan stole a look through the long grass and cow-parsley on the lip of the ditch. There were still people about. He couldn't get away. There was no rabbit-hole here for coat, flask, binoculars, partridges, net. Even deep in the ditch a dog would find them in a moment. The dew wasn't dry down in the shade of the ditch, and his scent and Pansy's would scream at a bloodhound.

Bloodhounds were Dan's greatest worry. But they didn't bring them. He heard the reason, from scraps of glum conversation above him. The police tracking-dogs, like the police themselves, were at full stretch over miles of country. A dozen farmers, defying AgriSecurity, had gone to the law, and the law was thin on the ground trying to protect them.

Dan had a long, long time to consider his own position. He was due that morning at the livery-stable, the beat-up establishment of the Hadfield sisters, to patch up the planking of some loose-boxes. They'd be angry when he didn't turn up. They might send to his cottage. That would worry his mother. Dan wondered how *she* was getting on, all on her own. She could get herself downstairs and make her own breakfast. She'd feed the birds and animals, let the bantams out, water the broodies. It would all leave her exhausted and in pain. Dan hoped she wouldn't try to make her bed or do the washing-up.

He heard a car bumping along the tractor-track at the edge of the stubble. He heard the Superintendent's voice. He must be nearly as short of sleep as Dan himself.

Another vehicle, a Land Rover, came crunching along the edge of the stubble.

The Superintendent's voice called, 'Bad business, Mr Mortimer.'

'Ay,' boomed Fred Mortimer's voice. 'What gets me is, the bastards seem to be telepathic. Three nights running we had a bloke watching this barley. Then old Jim Dodd gets trouble with the base of his spine, and straightaway they put a match to it.'

'Valuable crop?'

'The best on me land. Malting barley, under contract.'

'Insured?'

97

'Yes, thank God. As soon's I made the contract. April, that was, long before *this* business started.'

The maltsters couldn't have inspected the crop, Dan thought. It couldn't have been a firm contract – just a general intention to buy the grain, at a stated price, if it passed muster. That price, with the estimated yield, would have given the figure for the insurance. Presumably the insurers hadn't been to look at the crop, either. They'd accept Fred's figures, Fred being a good client who paid his premiums promptly.

Fred was a clever man, no doubt about that. He'd grown when everybody else was shrinking. He'd worked hard to grow, and now he was working hard to keep what he'd got. Fred was a good fellow, a hearty sporting old-fashioned type, what they used to call a substantial yeoman, what they still called the backbone of England. He was a cheat.

Cheat? The word had come into Dan's head, but he couldn't all at once account for it. Fred was set to cheat the insurance company, as Mr Calloway was doing, but that was just the way the rich stayed rich. It wasn't dishonest, it was self-defence, it was normal, they didn't think of it as cheating. There was something else on the edge of Dan's mind. He had a picture of Fred cheating in some game, some competition: as though he'd put his foot in front of the line in a darts match, pinched an extra ball when shying at coconuts, or claimed a bird he hadn't shot in a pheasant drive. But it wasn't quite that. Dan tried to remember what it was, but he was distracted by Pansy's impatient twitchings. Even she, the best-schooled dog in the world, was getting bored in the ditch. Maybe she was cramped, like Dan himself, or clammily uncomfortable in the heavy unevaporated dew.

The sun was getting high. There were no voices to be heard. A vehicle drove away

Pansy stirred. Her nostrils dilated under Dan's cheek. She was aware of something new, some new element nearby. Dan could hear nothing. He could smell only damp earth, and crushed, wet, minty vegetation under their bodies, and Pansy herself, and the acrid reek of the burned field. He could see only a tangle of dock and couch-grass and a bit of Pansy's flank. But Pansy's nose said something was happening, something new had arrived.

Dan heard a subdued but excited panting. He looked up cautiously, moving his head as little as possible. A black labrador was looking at them, sniffing, wagging his tail in friendly perplexity. Dan despised labradors for their sloppy, uncritical friendliness. He was not pleased with this one. Somebody would see it.

Somebody did.

'Hey, Blinker,' called Fred Mortimer's jolly voice, 'what ye got, boy? Come along, old boy.'

Blinker turned to Fred's call; he started obediently back towards the Land Rover, but turned again, sniffed, wagged his tail, enchanted to find dog and man in the ditch, wanting to make friends, wanting to love and be loved.

'Come here, you bloody runagate,' called Fred Mortimer.

Heavy boots crunched along the edge of the burned barley.

'Well now, well now,' said Fred. He was holding a pitchfork. 'I thought I'd prang a rabbit, but I see we got bigger game. Well now, Dan Mallett, what shall we do? Call the police back to pinch you for burning my barley, or prang you like a bunny with my fork?'

10

Fred Mortimer was six foot two; he was seventeen stone of hard, beef-fed sporting farmer. The heavy wooden handle of the pitchfork looked like a straw in his enormous red hand.

Dan, cramped, made a small movement, to relieve the arm he was lying on. Immediately one sharp prong of the pitchfork spiked at his diaphragm, just above his belt.

'Rest quiet,' said Fred Mortimer soothingly, 'before I spit ye like a straw-bale.'

Fred meant it. He had been killing farm-stock and poultry, wild animals and birds, all his life, as a large part of his life. Sudden death left him cold. He wouldn't hesitate a second to lean his weight on the pitchfork. Dan's belly clenched at the thought; all his skin crawled.

'I see how it was,' said Fred Mortimer, his great harvest-moon face wearing a sad smile. 'You needed the money for your mam. It does you credit, mebbe. Those were clever letters you wrote, or did you take on a seckyterry? But your methods when a bloke wouldn't pay, they were a bit crude, eh? You burned up me hay, fifty ton o' winter feed, 'cause I wouldn't pay. You poisoned the Doctor's trout, which must have been easy, you being a pal o' the keeper. You loosed off a bomb in Mr Calloway's glasshouse, 'cause he grabbed his money back. 'Cept he didn't. You know that? He showed me your letter, did Mr Calloway, and he never got the money at all. You was bloody-minded that time, Dan Mallett. That was nasty temper, that was. And now you burned me barley. It must ha' been you. Must ha' been. Else why are you here, eh? Why are you here? It's as clear as day, and the cops, they'll think so too.'

They would think so. Fred was dead right. Even if Dan showed them partridges and net, they'd still think he fired the barley. Where did that put him with the trout, the greenhouse, Fred's barn? With the letters and telephone calls? With extorting money with menaces?

Fred could haul Dan back to his farm and call the police. Or he could spit him with the pitchfork. Either would earn universal applause.

What Dan wanted now was a vicious collie like Willie Martin's, or a mastiff or bull-terrier or Alsatian, a dog who'd attack on command. Pansy was snappy, but she wouldn't attack. She was a dead loss in this situation. What else did Dan have, to match Fred's pitchfork, his position, his enormous size and strength?

Dan had never in his life felt less like smiling, but he compelled a broad smile to spread across his face. He intended it to express amazement, relief, triumph, deep satisfaction. He looked over Fred Mortimer's right shoulder, as though at a silent helicopter hovering there and full of his friends, or a balloon with a basketful of armed allies.

Fred was not fooled. His sad smile broadened into a fat grin. He beamed happily down at Dan, while Dan kept a fatuous smile pinned to his own face.

Dan wriggled the fingers of the hand hidden, by his body, from Fred. He grabbed a handful of Pansy's rough coat, and tweaked sharply. Pansy yelped and tried to jump. It might have been a yelp of excitement, instead of a squawk of pain and offended dignity. Dan widened his wide smile; he began to chuckle, excitedly greeting the silent helicopter over Fred's shoulder.

Dan's chuckle and Pansy's yelp were, together, too much for Fred. Involuntarily, for a fraction of a second, he took his eyes off Dan; he twisted his head to glance over his shoulder. Dan rolled away from under the prong of the pitchfork, freeing the arm he was lying on, freeing Pansy. He seized the bottom of the pitchfork with both hands, and jammed the prongs into the ground.

It did not take Fred long to pull the pitchfork out of the ground, but it was long enough for Dan. He scrambled out of the ditch, holding the partridge net, and danced out of range of the pitchfork. Pansy followed him, barking, pleased to be allowed to move. Fred lunged at Dan with the pitchfork, then swung it in a wide arc at the full stretch of his arms; the points whistled past an inch from Dan's chest.

'Curly!' bellowed Fred; his voice was loud enough to reach the village, rattle the windows of the pub, knock the churchyard yew trees out of the ground.

Fred's Land Rover was twenty yards away, behind Dan, on the tractor-track at the edge of the stubble. Had Fred left the key in the dash? Which way was it pointing? Was the gate at the bottom of the field closed or open? No one closed a gate on to stubble, but it might have swung shut of its own weight.

Fred yelled for Curly Godden. The yell was so loud that Curly must be some way off. Fred yelled only for Curly. That meant, with any luck, that Curly was the only person in earshot.

There was no time for Dan to turn round to see who was about, which way the Land Rover was pointing, whether the gate was shut. He was kept busy dancing clear of the long sharp prongs of the pitchfork. At the same time he was trying to unroll the partridge net, but the nylon mesh had caught round the ends of the bamboo spokes.

Fred bellowed wordlessly and came at Dan, jabbing mightily with the pitchfork. He had lost his temper. His great face was dark red and his mouth was open and dribbling. He was trying to kill Dan now. He'd forgotten any idea of getting the police: he was bent only on impaling Dan on the prongs of his pitchfork. He rushed at Dan, yelling, purple. Dan jumped aside. His feet tangled in Pansy; he tripped over her, and fell heavily sideways on the smoking barley field. Fred gave a bray of triumph, and lunged downwards at Dan's belly with the pitchfork. Dan, tangled with the yelping Pansy, rolled frantically over and over. The pitchfork plunged into the charred ground with all Fred's weight behind it. Dan jumped to his feet, tearing desperately at the nylon mesh of his net. By the time Fred had freed the pitchfork from the ground, Dan had torn away the snags in the net and shaken it wide open. Fred came at him again; Dan slammed the net over his head.

The net was strong stuff, but pretty light. Fred would claw his way through it in a second. A second was all Dan needed. He turned and ran for Fred's Land Rover. Fred thundered after him, dropping the deadly pitchfork, tearing at the net. Pansy barked and pranced like a fool, behaving quite unlike herself. The Land Rover was pointing the wrong way, up the track, away from Yewstop Lane. The big metal gate at the bottom of the stubble had swung shut. Dan jumped into the Land Rover. The key was there. He switched on and started, gunning the throttle, crashing stiffly into gear, lurching forward almost before he was properly in the driving seat.

Fred Mortimer, with tatters of the green netting hanging round him like seaweed, thundered up just as Dan got the Land Rover moving. He grabbed at the door handle and pulled the door open. Dan put his foot on the floor. The Land Rover's engine roared and it jumped forward over the bumps of the track. Fred lost his hold on the door; he fell and rolled on the ground; the Land Rover's rear wheel just missed him. Pansy tried to jump into the Land Rover, but bounced off the canvas at the back. Dan didn't dare stop to collect her. She'd get home. Dan swung the Land Rover in a tight circle, bumping violently over the stubble. He headed towards the gate. Fred, picking himself up off the ground, saw what he was doing. Fred ran towards the gate – to make sure, Dan thought, that it was fastened. It was a heavy tubular-steel cattle-gate, with a massive steel catch. The gateposts were girders of T-shaped iron, sunk in concrete. The track went through the gate over a culvert; there was a broad, deep ditch each side of the gate, the main runaway drain for a dozen acres. The Land Rover had to go through the gate – there was no other way for it to go.

Fred got to the gate a little before Dan, Dan a little before Pansy. The gate had swung shut but not latched itself; Fred latched it. A lot of heavy metal now barred Dan's way. He juddered to a halt a few yards short of the gate, and changed into four-wheel drive. He thumped into bottom gear and churned forward, the engine screaming as he put his foot hard down on the floor. Fred backed clear of the gateway, shouting incoherently. Dan smashed into the gate. Metal clanged and glass tinkled. The Land Rover stopped. All four wheels were spinning and the engine roaring. The gate was bent but still there. Catch and hinges had held. The metal gatepost at the hinges end was bent thirty degrees out of the vertical, but it had held too. Dan changed into reverse and charged backwards, hoping Pansy was out of the way. She was; she successfully jumped into the back of the Land Rover as Dan stopped again, changed gear, and roared forwards. He crunched into the gate. There was another rending of metal and shattering of glass. Fred Mortimer was scrabbling at the side of the Land Rover. The Land Rover's wheels bit; Dan kept his foot on the floor; the bent gatepost snapped at the base. The gate jumped out of hinges and catch. Dan charged forward with the bent metal gate hanging across the smashed front of the Land Rover.

He roared down the edge of the big pasture, through another gateway, across more stubble. He got to Yewstop Lane and turned right towards the main road. Suddenly Curly Godden was in front of him, his bicycle across the road. Dan put his hand on the horn-button and kept his foot on the floor. He hoped Curly wouldn't do anything heroic. Curly didn't. He jumped clear, deep into the hedge beside the road, only just missing the side of the gate on the Land Rover's radiator. He dropped his bicycle as he jumped. It fell on to the front of the Land Rover: on to the metal gate. The gate picked up the bicycle like the cowcatcher on a loco in a Western; a handlebar and a pedal stuck through the bars of the gate and held the bicycle there. Dan roared on, carrying Curly's bicycle and his coat and his sandwiches.

Dan was no more licensed to drive a car than he was to ride a motor-bike. He had never passed any test, or tried to do so. He told employers and people whose cars he borrowed that he had driven for twenty years without an endorsement or a conviction; it was true; he had also driven for twenty years without a licence. He was perfectly competent, though contemptuous of speed-limits.

Now Willie Martin's farm was on the left, with the river woods beyond, the main road ahead – and a police car behind. Dan heard its siren, then saw it in his wing mirror. Fred hadn't had time to get to a telephone, so this was pure bad luck. Curly would tell them to chase the Land Rover, if they weren't already doing so. They couldn't pass him in the lane, but they'd force him into the side in the main road.

It was possible they had dogs in the police car; they undoubtedly had a radio.

Willie Martin had a lot of sheep in a big pasture to Dan's left, ewes and full-grown lambs. Dan wondered how much Willie was paying AgriSecurity to keep the gates shut. That gave him the idea. He drove to the field gate, stopped beyond it, jumped out of the Land Rover. The police car, screaming, was 500 yards away. Dan opened the gate into the field and began driving the sheep out into the lane. They went in a series of rushes, in foolish panic, bumping into each other, getting jammed in the gateway. Within seconds there were dozens packed together in the lane, filling it, struggling. Pansy barked at the sheep. They fled away from her, back along the lane towards the oncoming police car. All the other sheep started following the first ones into the lane.

The police car screeched to a halt as it met the first terrified sheep. A wall of sheep faced it. Some tried to turn back, to run away from the police car, but the pressure of the flock behind drove them on at the car.

A police driver wouldn't run over a flock of sheep.

Dan jumped back into the Land Rover and drove it fast towards the main road. The police behind would have radio'd by now. Another police car would come and cut him off, but not for a minute or two, unless his luck had run out.

It hadn't. He drove home as fast as he could. A couple of people saw him and laughed, but there was no police car or road block.

His mother was feeding the bantams outside the cottage. Her face looked white and tired, but it lit up when she saw him.

'All right?' she said. Peering at the Land Rover, she added, 'What's this, then? A bulldozer?'

'No time to explain,' said Dan. 'I'm going off for a day or two. Don't worry, old lady. We'll be back to normal by-long an' by-late.'

'Your Dad all over again,' sighed his mother. 'I 'speck you want me to feed the zoo.'

'It would be charitable,' said Dan apologetically.

He had to get away, but not far away. If the police caught him now he'd be arrested and remanded in custody. Then they'd build their case, with help from Doctor Smith, Fred Mortimer, Curly Godden and Mr Calloway. Maybe Camilla, too, who wouldn't want to help, but might be tricked or bullied into doing so. The police wouldn't believe anything his mother said about him, and they wouldn't believe anything he said about himself, not after Fred had found him hiding in the ditch by the fire. The police trusted Fred. He was well in with them – they told him everything. Dan had to go away, but not far away. He had to be near enough to get himself out of trouble. To prove who AgriSecurity was.

First things first. He pitched Pansy out of the Land Rover and into her kennel. He ran indoors. He took the partridges out of his coat and tossed them on the kitchen table. For all her disapproval, his mother knew enough to pluck them quick and say they were bantams. He ran upstairs and threw a few things into a duffle-bag. It occurred to him that he might want some sort of disguise, so he packed his neat blue suit, his banker's shoes, a clean white shirt and dark tie. He trotted away into

Priory Wood, not having been at home for as long as ten minutes. At least his mother knew he was all right.

The police would assume he'd get as far away as possible, as quick as possible. They'd watch all the roads for the Land Rover. They'd come to the cottage. Finding the Land Rover, what would they think? That he'd stolen a car, thumbed a ride, borrowed a horse, taken a bus? They'd have to explore all those possibilities. Meanwhile there'd be a warrant out for him, a description circulated. They'd search the cottage. They wouldn't find anything terrible – no silver, no money, not his shotgun or rifle. His mother wouldn't tell them anything.

Dan pushed his way through Priory Wood, keeping an ear out for dogs. It was honeycombed with rabbit-warrens, badger-setts, foxes' earths, with hiding-places used by Dan and by his father before him. The place was not keepered like the Major's or the river woods. The syndicate that had the shooting was too far away to supervise things. It was hardly worth either shooting or poaching. The roe-deer were the best things in it; a haunch made a lovely little roast.

On the far side of the wood he crossed a road carefully, went through another small wood, and came out on the edge of the Priory park, now the playing fields of the Medwell Priory School. Of course the little girls were all away now, on their summer holidays. Nobody was in the house except Jake and Ruby Collis the caretakers, maybe a teacher or two in cottages near, a few gardeners and the like. Jake and Ruby were the only problem. They were no friends of Dan's. Ruby gave herself airs. She was far above an odd-job man. She was a trained sec-retary. She'd had a job in the betting-shop in Milchester. Then she married Jake, a bit sudden, which was a come-down. But she still gave herself airs.

The Priory itself was a great, gaunt, hideous house built of purple brick and Portland stone in about 1900. Its huge high rooms and stoneflagged corridors were cold even in the height of summer; there was a funny smell throughout. The atmosphere filled Dan with gloom; it was like being in an ugly cold town.

But he knew his way round the attics and cellars. He knew he could hide there for ever, bloodhounds or no bloodhounds.

Dan approached cautiously; he didn't want to be seen from an upstairs window. He got to the wall of the main house, vaulted an area railing, and slipped in through a basement window. He was in what looked like a communal shower, smelling of antiseptic soap; he tried, but failed, to picture it full of splashing naked little girls.

Going always cautiously, constantly stopping and listening, he crept up through the house, by great gaunt rooms once grand, now reduced to the shabby misery of classrooms; and further up to the servants' attic bedrooms, now full of small beds with identical baby-blue coverlets. There was everything here he needed – privacy, modern plumbing, and, with a little effort, something to eat. If he was tidy and careful nobody would know he was here, and nobody would know he'd ever been here.

He drew back one of the coverlets in a little attic dormitory, and lay down on the bed, sighing deeply. It was a little bed, a young child's bed, but it was big enough for Dan. There were no sheets, of course, but there were folded blankets and a pillow without a pillowcase. It was not as comfortable as his bed at home, but it was much more comfortable than last night's ditch.

Dan was tired but wakeful. His brain went round and round. He was deeply puzzled. He knew what was happening. With a few gaps, he knew how it was being done. What he couldn't understand was why. He found himself wishing, in a most uncharacteristic way, that he was the sort of person who could go to the police and tell them everything he knew.

But even if that was possible, they wouldn't think he knew what he thought he knew. They had a different meaning for 'know'. He was getting together bits of proof, but none of it was what they'd call proof. They'd think he was mad, and lock him up all the quicker.

He had to know more, what they'd call know. He had to get what the police thought was proof, or else blow AgriSecurity sky-high, on his own. He had to do it without getting murdered or arrested.

He'd been lucky not to be arrested earlier in the day. He'd been lucky not to be murdered, too. Falling over Pansy like that, with Fred Mortimer charging up like a maddened dairy bull, and almost as big . . . Funny chap, Fred. For all his strength and grossness and violent temper and snobbery, he could be as gentle as a sweet old lady, as Dan's mother. Dan remembered him at a Beautiful Baby contest in the Medwell Village Hall, two years before, all amongst the Vicar and the twittering local ladies, holding the winning baby, clucking at it like a hen with one chick . . .

Cheat. That was it. Fred had cheated. They'd had a judging panel for the Beautiful Babies. Five judges. Mrs Potter was one of them. Fred was the Chairman of the panel. He liked that sort of job because he liked being the bluff old squire. Fred had fudged the voting. Nobody noticed except Dan, who had a suspicious mind, and picked up the voting-slips afterwards.

Why? The prize was nothing – a knitted baby cardigan, a teddy-bear. Had somebody bribed Fred to see their baby won? Not possible. None of the village people had enough money to interest Fred, and the nobs with the money didn't enter their babies in contests. Besides, the nobs in the neighbourhood were long past babies. It must have been important to Fred himself.

Whose baby was it? Dan had no recollection. It wasn't a couple in the village itself. But local. You wouldn't travel a distance to enter a baby in a contest, not for a woolly or a soft toy.

Dan sighed deeply again, lying on his back on the hard, twanging child's bed. He shrugged mentally. There were more important things to think about.

AgriSecurity was going to make another demand on the Calloways. Camilla would know about it. He must keep in touch with Camilla. There were dozens of other demands, maybe scores, that he didn't know about: but he knew about that one, and it was all he had to go on.

His whole body began to ache with fatigue when he thought about crawling in cover all the way to the Calloways', maybe to find Camilla had gone to London for the day. Then he remembered that, for once, he was living in a house with a telephone: probably dozens of telephones.

He got up stiffly, tidied the little bed, and crept out and downstairs. He successfully avoided Jake Collis, who was using an electric floor-polisher on the parquet of a first-floor room. He avoided Ruby, who was on her way out to go shopping. Peeping from a window, he watched Ruby bicycle away down the drive. As long as he heard the whine of the polisher, he knew he was safe from Jake.

Instinct or memory took him along a back passage to a little dark room, an office, with filing-cabinets and photographs of women's cricket-teams. On a scarred desk were not only a telephone but also a local directory.

He dialled the Calloways' number. Old Mrs Calloway answered. Dan filled his mouth with imaginary marbles, and asked for Camilla Calloway.

'Who is speaking, please?'

'Hubert Cavendish,' said Dan, tugging at a moustache and adjusting a monocle in his eye.

'Hullo,' said Camilla presently. She was panting a little, as though she had run in from the garden.

'Morning,' said Dan. 'I've been missing you something horrible.'

She giggled and said, 'Oh Hubert! How nice to hear your voice.'

She was quick on the uptake. She was able to tell him, without seeming to do so, that AgriSecurity had not yet made its demand. But all the arrangements stood, which meant that the money was ready.

'Any chance of seeing you, Hubert?' chirruped Camilla.

'Night-time would be best,' said Dan.

'It's a bit complicated,' said Camilla cleverly. 'My parents-in-law are going out to dinner tomorrow night, but I've got to be here in case Miss Hadfield comes about the pony . . .'

That was fixed, then.

'The police are looking for you,' said Camilla in a different voice. Evidently she was no longer being overheard.

'I know,' said Dan.

'Where are you?'

'Oh, miles away. A long way away. But I'll see you tomorrow night. Will you be riding Cherry tomorrow?'

'I expect so,' she said, surprised. 'Why?'

'Can I ask a big favour? Could you ride past my cottage? Anyone will tell you where it is. It's just to see if my mother's all right. She won't want any help, but she might have fallen downstairs . . .'

Camilla said she'd be delighted to ride that way, to meet Dan's mother. They hung up. Dan listened for Jake's floor-polisher, and heard it whining far away.

He had another idea. He dialled Mrs Potter at the Old Mill.

'Hullo,' she said, her voice self-conscious and actressy.

'This is Jake Ruby, of the *Milchester Argus*,' said Dan.

'Oh yes,' said Mrs Potter avidly.

Dan said he was preparing an illustrated feature on village life in the Milchester area. He understood there were Beautiful Baby contests in Medwell Fratrorum and that, two years previously, Mrs Potter had been one of the judges.

'Yes indeed,' said Mrs Potter. 'One does everything one can to help.'

She said she would be delighted to pose for an *Argus* photographer.

'And the child?' said Dan. 'Do you remember the winner?'

'Why yes. Quite a bonny little thing. I did not vote for her myself, but we were a committee, you know, quite democratic. The child was called Karen Yeo. A nice clean baby, perhaps overweight.'

'Ah,' said Dan. 'We'd like her picture too. Do you know where the parents live, Mrs Potter?'

'Yes indeed. They were quite humble people. They live in

Ighampton, or did. I remember because there was a feeling that a stranger should not win our local contest. We old-fashioned country people are inclined to be parochial, I'm afraid.'

Dan thanked Mrs Potter, and promised again to come and photograph her. She crooned that he and the photographer would be welcome at any time.

Yeo. Their child had a connection with Fred Mortimer. Any oddity about Fred was worth looking at just now, and this was definitely an oddity.

There was a dozen Yeos in the local telephone book. One lived in Ighampton, at 44 Heath Road. Dan knew Heath Road, which was part of a big council estate. It was obviously the right thing to go there, and there was no point in delay. He had to have a reason to knock on the door and ask questions. He decided to be a man from the Council, some kind of official. They were always calling on the tenants, bothering them, frightening them, coddling them. That meant blue suit, clean collar, little black shoes. He had thought he might eventually want those things; he wanted them immediately.

He crept away to wash, shave, and put his smart clothes on. Jake was still polishing the floor.

On his way downstairs again – every inch a bank manager or a senior Council official – Dan reflected that the Yeos in the telephone book might be the wrong ones. The right ones, if humble people, might not have a telephone. There was an easy way to find out.

Dan went back to the little office and dialled the Yeos' number.

After only one ring the telephone was picked up the other end. A high parrot voice, deafeningly loud, squawked into Dan's ear, 'Hullo! Hullo! Hullo! Hullo! Hullo!'

Dan realized it was a young child. He said loudly, 'Can I speak to your mam?'

'Hullo-hullo-hullo-hullo-*hullo*,' screamed the child.

'Can I speak to Mrs Yeo?' shouted Dan.

The child began to cry, and hung up. Dan sighed. He was

about to dial the number again when he glanced up and saw Ruby Collis standing in the door. She had a basket in her hand and a scarf round her head; she was staring at him pop-eyed.

'That's a shockin' liberty, Dan Mallett,' she screeched. 'Who d'you think you are, coming in bold as brass and using a private phone? I'll have the police on you, see if I don't.'

'You did your shopping very quick, Ruby,' said Dan mildly.

'Forgot my list. Never mind that. Get away from the phone so I can ring for the police.'

'I'll cut the cord,' said Dan, taking his knife from his pocket and flicking out the larger blade.

'Threaten me with a dagger, would you?' screamed Ruby. She ran out, shouting for Jake.

Dan sighed. It seemed highly likely the child he had heard was Karen, the baby-contest winner, the one Fred Mortimer had cheated for. The thing to do was go there. He trotted out of the house by a small back door into a yard. A woman's bicycle was leaning on the wall by the door: Ruby's. Dan jumped on to it and sped away down the back drive.

He took a route to Ighampton which combined footpath, bridle-path, farm-track, and, for 200 yards, dry stream bed. He crossed a couple of roads; he saw a police car on each.

Ruby Collis, he thought, wouldn't actually call the police. Jake would get her off the idea. He wasn't actually very sensible, but he was more sensible than Ruby. As far as they knew, all he'd done was come in and use a telephone. You might be annoyed about that, but you didn't bother the police about it: especially if it wasn't your telephone bill. Unless, of course, they knew the police were looking for Dan. He could see no reason why they should know. If they had known, Ruby would have said something.

Even if they did ring, what had Ruby heard? Only 'Yeo'. There were a dozen Yeos in the book, spread over a big area.

Mrs Potter wouldn't report her call to the police: why should she? She might, after a fortnight's disappointment, ring the *Milchester Argus*. That would start a few hares. But by that time Dan would have won, or be in gaol, or be dead.

The house was a new, five-room semi in a cul-de-sac on a big council estate, a miniature new town with no privacy, plenty of cars, and a forest of TV aerials.

The Yeos' bell went ding-dong; a thin woman of thirty-five answered it. She had a gentle, exhausted face. She wore an apron over a decent dress. She had tried to make her hair look smart, but it was against her.

'Mrs Yeo?'

'Yes? Are you selling anything? We got everything.'

A sturdy child, a girl of three, stumped into the small hall-way. She was big-limbed, well fed, obviously healthy, expensively overdressed.

'Is that little Karen?' said Dan.

'Me,' shouted Karen. She continued to shout 'Me! Me! Me!' She was hysterical and maybe retarded.

'Are you from the Welfare?' asked Mrs Yeo.

'Education Department,' said Dan, who had planned his tactics as he travelled. 'Can I have a minute of your time?'

'Come in,' she said without enthusiasm.

She led him into an opulently furnished sitting-room, very tidy, with an enormous colour TV. There was a children's programme on the TV; watching it was a grey-faced man in bedroom slippers. He started to get up when Dan came in, but a spasm of pain crossed his face and he sat back helplessly.

'My husband,' said Mrs Yeo, turning off the television. 'He sticks like that, gets jammed. Disc. Nothing seems to help. Bob, this is Mr –'

'Calloway,' said Dan. 'Sorry to trouble you –'

'No trouble,' said Bob Yeo. 'Glad of a diversion.'

'We're doing a survey,' said Dan, 'about, hum, future educational needs. School places, like.'

'Yer, well. Karen's goin' to need a special school. We been into it with the Welfare. There's nothing suitable locally, so she'll prob'ly go to a private school, fee-payin'.'

'Oh,' said Dan, very surprised. 'None of my business, but with you off work –'

'You talkin' about the money? That's no problem. The mother sees to that.'

'The mother?' said Dan, baffled for a moment.

'Karen's a foster,' said Mrs Yeo without expression. 'We can't have any, so . . .'

'Adopted?'

'No. We would, but the mother won't have it.'

'Ah,' said Dan. Carefully he went on, 'The natural mother's name will, of course, be on file at the office, but to save everybody trouble can I ask you – ?'

'Janice King,' said Bob Yeo. 'We keeps it a secret hereabouts, but like you say, it's all on paper at the Council.'

'Ah,' said Dan, pieces falling into place in his mind like the parts of a dismantled shotgun. 'Love-child?'

'O' course. We don't know who the father is. She does, but we don't.'

'Her present address?' said Dan. 'Of course that's on file at the office, too, but . . .'

'We don't know,' said Mrs Yeo. 'And I bet it's not on file in any office. She moves around. The last letter was from London, care of a newsagent. We don't know what she does, exactly –'

'She's a –' Bob Yeo glanced round, saw that Karen was not listening, and whispered, 'tart.'

'We don't know that, Bob,' said his wife reproachfully.

'Near enough,' said Bob. 'How else does she come by all that money?'

Dan made his visit credible by a few more questions about Karen. There was something badly wrong with the child mentally, although she was as strong as a little bear physically. It was too soon to say how backward she was, how much she could ever be taught.

He saw round the house. It was as expensively furnished as the Calloways', though in a different style.

'The mother's generous,' said Mrs Yeo, 'whatever else.'

'This is all new?'

'Yes. We done it room by room. The cash come from London, *in* cash.'

'You banking some for the kid?'

'The mother says not to. Says she's doing all the needful there, the special school and all.'

Janice, the neat little dark one, with a turned-up nose and greedy eyes. Janice, that Dan himself could have fancied, but never got round to trying. Janice, Fred Mortimer's farm secretary, who disappeared suddenly three years ago, causing talk, like anything did, whether there was fire under the smoke or not.

There was fire this time, sure enough, but was it so terrible? Fred's wife was long dead. Why didn't he look after his own? He loved the child, to the point of cheating in the contest. He didn't want to acknowledge little Karen: didn't want anyone to know the scandal. But was it so scandalous, these days? Would the nobs turn their backs on Fred because he had a little bastard and looked after it? Was he ashamed because Karen was retarded?

He said good-bye to the Yeos and to Karen. Karen shouted at him mindlessly. No wonder her foster-mother looked tired. They were good people, though they lived in a council house stuffed with overpriced, ugly, brand-new furniture, with televisions and electrical gadgets.

They thought it was the wages of sin. It was more like the wages of death.

Dan went out into the well-barbered cul-de-sac of neat new semis. He thought it was a horrible place. Two hundred yards away the quiet side-street debouched into a larger one, lined with exactly similar houses. There was no other way out. At the corner, surrounded by curious children, sat a police car.

11

So Ruby did ring the police, and they picked the right Yeo. No – the police would have brought the car to the door, not parked it two hundred yards away.

That car wasn't after Dan at all. It was there on different business. Dan's best plan was to get on Ruby's bicycle and sail out of the side-street with a happy expression. Oh no, oh no. There was a warrant out for him. The police in the car would have had his description. They might be there on other business, but they'd keep an eye out for Dan too. Ruby's bike as well, a fierce and distinctive mauve, with a matching mauve basket on the front. It was madness to go near the car, on wheels or on foot.

It was no good going back through the Yeos'. She'd see the police car when she came to the door, couldn't fail to realize he was trying to avoid it. Especially if he said he wanted to go out through the back, leaving the bike at the front. They'd be on to the police the minute his back was turned, law-abiding people like that. Anyway the back door led nowhere, only to a strip of garden. Beyond the garden, all along the back of the council estate, there was an eight-foot fence of new red planking. If Dan hopped over that, thirty people would see him.

No – not quite. Three houses along from the Yeos', a foot-path ran between gardens. There must be a gap, gate, stile in the Council's fine new fence. Dan strolled along to the foot-path. It was a little gritty path of baked dirt, chain-link on each side stretched on metal fence-posts; nettles luxuriated at both edges of the path, though the gardens beyond the chain-link looked as though they were kept tidy with dustpan-and-brush and nail-scissors. Responsibility stopped at the fence. At the end of thirty yards of path there was just a gap in the wooden fence. Beyond there seemed to be nothing but scrubby waste ground, a dry jungle of brambles and nettles and bindweed. Presumably a footpath led through it; if not, no matter.

Dan sauntered up the path, as though he had a little time to kill and a whim to explore. He paused in the gap in the fence. The strip of waste ground was a miserable sight – good farmland, let go, now useless and squalid and ugly. It was obvious what had happened, because the same thing happened in so many places. Using powers of compulsory purchase, and delighted to be spending the ratepayers' money, the Council had bought more land than it needed. This waste was the spare, the left-overs, ten acres, six or eight thousand quids' worth when the land was still used. The sun glared everywhere on bright objects in the undergrowth, bottles, tin cans, bits of beat-up perambulators, the springs of broken furniture. Fields of decent arable or grazing had become the council tenants' rubbish dump.

There was a winding, well-trodden path through the jungle, made by the rubbish-dumpers when they crept out at night. It might not reach the lane beyond the waste ground, but for a while it made the going easier. Dan started down the path. The ground dipped. Mounds of vicious bramble rose high behind him, impenetrable on both sides. He was out of sight of the council houses, out of sight of anybody. There was still a kind of path, hardly more than a rabbit-track.

Something snapped a few yards behind. Dan turned quickly. A big man was extricating himself unhurriedly from a kinder patch of undergrowth, a knoll of dry grass; he moved gracefully, like a dancer, even in this awkward process. Dan recognized him from his movements. He was wearing a big, shiny, spherical crash-helmet, although Dan had borrowed his motor-bike. He carried a slasher, a heavy curved billhook on a four-foot handle. He came two yards towards Dan; now he filled the narrow path, a wall of dense brambles each side of him. There was no way past him except over the top.

The man's face was strange to Dan, who had seen him only in the dark and with a scarf round his head. It was an ordinary face, except for buck teeth under which a thick lower lip was caught. The effect was childish. His face was solemn, determined; he was not ferocious, not enjoying himself either, but engaged on an important job which he had no intention of scamping.

Dan turned forward again, knowing what he was going to see. He saw it. Two men were on the path in front of him. The nearest was a complete stranger to Dan, another big man in blue overalls and heavy boots; he had a big face with small features crowded all together in the middle. There was no glee on his face, and no reluctance. He held an identical slasher, the sun gleaming on the sharpened edge of the hook.

Behind him stood a much smaller man with a bandaged wrist. Dan didn't know the face but he knew the wrist; he would know the voice, too. The little man held a pair of long-handled pruning shears. He had a small, ratty face, and a small moustache.

'Nosey Parker,' said the small man. 'See where it gets you.'

'How did you know I'd be here?' asked Dan, really wanting to know.

'We knew.'

Who told them? Ruby Collis?

'How did you know I'd come this way?' asked Dan.

'No other way you could,' said the little man triumphantly. 'We tip off the fuzz there was goin' to be an empty house robbed. So they stake it out, see? We knew you wouldn't go near it. That left this road, the on'y road you 'ad.'

'Very clever,' said Dan. 'What do you want to do – talk?'

'Slice you up into bits.' He waved the pruning shears at the horrible tangles of undergrowth. 'The bits can bide here.'

They could, too. Once Dan's body was deep in the stuff, it was lost until the Council decided to build more houses.

'Why?' asked Dan mildly. 'What you got against me?'

'Nothin',' said the little man. 'I never heard o' you, till the boss phones half an hour ago. Said you was comin' 'ere. We jumps into a car, an' it all worked out lovely. Just orders, chum. No hard feelin's.'

'I'll give you some money,' said Dan. 'A lot of money.'

'I doubt it,' said the little man. 'If you got a lot o' money on you now, we'll find it in a minute.'

'It's not on me. It's hidden.'

'Yah. Tell yer grandmother.'

'If somebody's havin' me killed,' said Dan, 'you might tell me who. Also why.'

'Fair enough,' said the little man handsomely. 'No 'arm that I can see. 'Cep we dunno. Honest. Tell you if I could, seein' it's the last thing you'll 'ear. But it's jus' a voice on the phone. As to *why*, its like I said, you're a Nosey Parker. That's all the boss said. He says " 'E's on the run from the fuzz, so get a fuzz-car there an' 'e'll bolt the opposite way. 'E's a Nosey Parker an' I want 'im dead." 'E describes you exact, an' 'e says you'll be goin' into Number 44. Which you done. Satisfied? That's all I can tell you, chum.'

'Get on, do,' said the high voice of the man in the crash-helmet.

Dan's only chance was to do the unexpected. Go for the two men, not the one. Then go back towards the police, not out into the open country. Dan reached into his coat, pulled out Sir George Simpson's flask, and flung it at the small man. Not much of the small man was visible behind the bigger man in front of him; the target was narrow and moving; Dan almost missed it. But the heavy flask, silver lined with thick glass, bounced off the small man's temple. The small man yelped and staggered. He was not knocked out. The big man in front of him glanced back over his shoulder. Impossible not to, like Fred when Pansy yelped. Dan saw a shadow, on the wall of brambles, running up behind him. It was the man with the crash-helmet, not seven feet away, swinging the heavy steel slasher on its four-foot handle. A man straddled his legs to do that, any man, always, to keep his balance and get power behind the swing. Dan dropped to a crouch, turning, making himself as small as a rabbit, and propelled himself like a rabbit between the straddled legs of the attacker.

The man was fast; his reactions were quick; he turned and started after Dan before Dan was many yards clear. The other big man, both other men, crashed after him. Dan sped up the track and through the gap in the fence. The police car might easily have gone. He ran along the footpath between the gardens, slowed to a walk, and emerged on to the quiet side-road.

The police car was still there, 200 yards away.

Dan heard the boots of the men behind him, crunching through the dry jungle, then pounding on the hard dirt of the footpath.

They couldn't chop him into slices with their slashers out there in the road, watched by dozens of kids and two policemen in a car. But it suited them very well if he was arrested. He still didn't know anything, not to say *know*. He still wouldn't be believed, not a word he said. He could be killed another time, if need be; meanwhile, behind bars, he could do them no harm. So they'd chivvy him down, a pack of dogs with one sheep, towards the sleek white car on the corner.

Dan strolled down towards the police car, since there wasn't any other way to go. He could see the two uniformed policemen in the peaked caps with the checked bands. They looked young and keen and alert. They were chatting to the children clustered round the car, but they were keeping an eye out too. They hadn't noticed Dan. But they soon would. Nothing could prevent them.

Dan glanced behind. All three men had come out of the footpath on to the road. They carried their tools like tools, not like weapons; they were Council employees knocking off after clearing some brambles from the waste ground. They blocked Dan's exit. If Dan stopped, they'd convoy him down to the police and hand him over; or simply make sure they saw him.

In despair, Dan glanced to his left, across the over-neat garden of the semi he was passing. Through an open window he saw a fat young woman watching television. Outside the house, on the shaven lawn, was a pram with a baby in it.

Dan borrowed the baby.

He trundled the pram briskly down the side-road, clucking at the baby who was lying in it. He waved to the alert young policemen, who ignored him; they were looking for wanted criminals, not bank managers with prams. Some of the children looked surprised – they probably knew the pram – but they didn't say anything to the policemen. There was a hoarse shout from behind, but Dan carried on. He rounded the corner into the larger road. Two vans were parked ten yards away, facing away from him. One was a baker's van, one a dairy's electric float. The baker wasn't delivering, not to council houses; the driver must live here. The dairy might be delivering, even at this time of day; if so the key was in the dash.

Dan glanced back. The men were near. They could get him by shouting 'Stop thief!' but, being crooks, it didn't occur to them. They split up. Crash-helmet was standing on the corner, near the police car. The others crossed the road. The small one kept level with Dan, the big one in overalls trotted forward to cut him off. Dan was still in full view of the police car.

He went on past the baker's van and parked the pram in front of it. The pram was now invisible to the policemen. He kicked on the brake that held the pram safely motionless. As he did so the milk-float started. Its battery-driven motor pulled it along very slowly, making a humming noise. The driver had been at the wheel all the time; Dan had not seen him.

Dan jumped on to the back and clung. The baker's van still hid him from the police car. The milk-float itself hid him from the man who had gone on ahead, but he was in full view of the other two.

They must have wondered, for a second, what to do. They did what Dan would have done – gave chase at full speed. They could run faster than the little electric motor could drive, and the driver would stop at the main road anyway.

The small man with the pruning-shears was the first to get

to the float. He was shouting to the driver, but the rattle of milk-bottles drowned his shouts. He swung the big shears at Dan. Dan pulled a full pint milk-bottle out of a metal crate in the open back of the float; clinging to the float with his left hand, he brought it down as hard as he could on the small man's head. The bottle broke. The man was masked in a flood of creamy white. He sagged at the knees and collapsed in a lake of milk.

The man with the crash-helmet came on, swinging his slasher. He was shouting to the driver of the float and to his friend in front. The float was going quite fast now and the milk-bottles rattled deafeningly. Dan pulled another milk-bottle out of the crate and shied it at the man with the crash-helmet. It missed and exploded in the road. He shied another. Instinctively the pursuer swung at it with his slasher, like a baseball player, in-stead of simply ducking. He hit it. The heavy steel head of the slasher smashed the bottle. Milk and glass flew all over the man. Broken glass probably got into his eyes; milk certainly did. He bellowed.

The driver of the float had stayed unaware of what was going on, what with the noise of the rattling bottles and concentrating on his driving, and Dan being too light for him to notice the extra weight. But now he saw the third man waving madly at him to stop. Peering round the back of the float, Dan saw the man waving, shouting, holding his slasher above his head. The float stopped.

Dan shied half a dozen full milk-bottles, one after the other, as far as he could forward, towards the man with the slasher. They landed and exploded, one after the other, in full view of the driver. The driver screamed and jumped out of his driving seat. He ran round to the back of the float. At the same time Dan ran round to the front, on the other side, ducking low below the high-piled milk-bottles. Dan jumped into the driving seat and started the float. He drove straight at the man with the slasher, who stood his ground for a moment, then leapt aside as nimbly as Curly Godden. Dan accelerated to the utmost, but the float was slow gathering speed. He swung into the main road without slowing down. Brakes screamed behind him. The tail of the float seemed to swing far out with the turn, and there was shouting from behind just audible over the rattling bottles. Dan realized that the driver and the attacker were both clinging to the back of the float, as he had done.

He heard the police car's siren, which he had been expecting for several seconds.

He swung the float at full speed into the parking-space in front of a grocer's shop. There were a dozen cars parked there, a bare space for the float between two of them. The bottles rattled like a million teeth when he jammed on the brakes. He was tight between two cars, having barely room to squeeze out. He edged clear and ran round the back of the grocery into a yard full of flies and crates and dustbins. There was a chorus of shouting from the road, a hue and cry. The police car screamed up and stopped.

But Dan was all right now. He was out of sight, he could stay out of sight. He was a fox being hunted in a country with open drains and unstopped earths: he could save his brush for sure.

He vaulted a rickety fence between the grocer's yard and a garden. The garden was unkempt and squalid. By the back door of a cottage an old woman was stringing beans. She looked up and stared at Dan through dim, piggy eyes.

'Read the meter, ma'am,' said Dan respectfully.

'A lad cam', the other day.'

'He made a mistake, he did. Overchargin' you.'

'Bleedin' amachews. How d'ye get in there, eh?'

'Short cut from grocer's.'

'What's them yells? Oo's yellin'?'

'Smash an' grab. Young lad pinched a can o' peaches.'

'Don't blame un. I likes a peach.'

'You *are* a peach,' said Dan gallantly.

'Sauce-box,' she said, delighted.

'Ta-ta, then,' said Dan, and trotted into the cottage.

'Meter's in kitchen,' his new friend called after him.

The cottage smelled of ancient damp, cobwebs, soot and feet. Dan went out of the front. It was one of a terrace, a mean little row opposite the disused railway station. There was nobody about. Most of the cottages were condemned, derelict, empty; their tenants had been moved to the fine new housing estate where the Yeos lived. Dan climbed into the station yard, which was sprouting grass and willow-herb. He went on to the platform and down on to the tracks. He crossed the four tracks, stepping carefully over the live rails. Beyond the station was the main road to Milchester; Dan crossed it quickly, looking for police cars. Then he set off across country for Medwell.

To be killed for being a Nosey Parker, was he? For finding out about little Karen? But what was so incriminating about one retarded three-year-old child?

Was Fred so ashamed of a half-witted bastard that he'd have a man murdered to keep the secret?

Ruby hadn't rung the police, she'd rung Fred. She was another one, then, that Fred had a hold over. It wouldn't do to be seen by them again.

Dan went on thinking as he walked.

AgriSecurity was in no hurry to get Mr Calloway's £500. Why not? Obviously because they were busy. The available men were picking up other payoffs, or failing to do so. Either way, they rang the boss. If all had gone well, that was it. They were told where to leave the money. If not, they were told to poison fish or let off bombs. They rang a number, a number they all knew, and delivered reports and got instructions. That telephone must be pretty busy in the small hours of the morning.

Dan thought that if he could get the telephone number he could plant a bomb of his own.

He had intended to go back to the Priory, where he thought he'd be safest. But he changed direction. He set off, not at all happily, for the one place which really frightened him.

12

Coxmore had once been a small manor house, in the days when
the minor gentry could live gentry-like on the rents of 200
acres. That was long ago. Now the gentry lived on London
salaries, tax fiddles, expense accounts and overdrafts. Coxmore
House became Coxmore Farm. But after 200 years Fred
Mortimer had made it grand again. He had built on consider-
ably, in a style not everyone liked. There was a lot of window
glass in his new wing, and the rest was not brick or stone but
wood. People said it was Scandinavian, but to Dan it looked
like boatbuilding. The outbuildings were like a village. They
came all kinds. Some were thatched. There were three huge
ricks of straw beside the farmyard, and a Dutch barn full of
hay.

The farmyard was still bustling when Dan got there in the
early evening. Trailers were being dragged in with sacks or
bales: Fred had a fork-lift truck stacking them. Huge Swiss-
rolls of straw, made by the new kind of baler, were sitting in
a row by the ricks. It was a cheerful, prosperous scene – a
highly efficient mechanized farm bringing in the last of its
prodigious harvest.

Fred Mortimer's voice would bellow louder than any, when
they sang their hymns of thanksgiving at the Harvest Festival.
Then he'd take the plate round, while his oafish sons tried to
make eyes at the girls.

Dan crawled round to the back of the house, keeping very
low, very anxious not to be seen. Peeping through a lavender
hedge, he saw old Glad Fowler busy in the kitchen. She was
probably making a late cold supper for the family. At some

stage she'd start carrying it through. She did, opening a door with her foot, tottering under the weight of a laden tray.

Dan had never been inside the house. Fred would no more have employed him than he would have asked him to dinner. He knew nothing about the layout of the house. He'd heard there were some fine things there, things Fred had bought, antique furniture and sporting pictures and silver. It had never occurred to Dan to consider trying for any of that, even in his new career, even to raise the £1,200. Fred was a far cry from people like the Calloways or the Potters, not a man to take chances with, a different cup of tea altogether.

In the house at the moment were Fred himself, his two teen-aged sons home from school for the holidays, and old Glad Fowler who had been in the woodwork, like a beetle, since Dan could remember.

Almost certainly Fred had a burglar alarm. He was that sort of man. Certainly there was at least one dog, Blinker the labrador; probably others. The boys might have terriers, spaniels, whippets. There was no outside kennel, surprisingly, and no farm-dog on a chain in the yard.

Maybe Fred liked going to and fro at odd hours, without rousing the household. There were painted women in Milchester, to comfort a lusty widower; he'd go and see them in his Bentley.

There the Bentley was, and three other cars. Fred's Land Rover was not there; it was having its nose banged back into shape. Curly's bicycle never would get back into shape; no doubt Fred had already bought him another, as he couldn't do his job without. Fred being Fred, the price was probably stopped out of Curly's wages

Dan detested the idea of walking into Fred Mortimer's house in broad daylight. But he emerged from the shrubbery and slipped through the open back door. He was in a stone-flagged passage by the kitchen. From the passage rose a steep wooden flight of back stairs. He went up them fast; they creaked, but Glad was rattling plates, and there was a lot of noise from the farmyard. He went into the new glass-and-wood part of the house, and carefully opened a door. As he expected it was a big, well-furnished bedroom, neat, not in use, a guest-room; it stood ready for the snobbish daughter and her military husband, or Fred's grand shooting friends; it stood ready for Dan.

There was a fitted cupboard he could hide in, and a bed he could hide under, and a nice deep chintzy chair he could sit in. Maybe later, much later, he could take a drink off Fred Mortimer.

The bustle in the farmyard subsided. Vehicles were parked and switched off. Cars and bicycles went away. The Mortimers came in. Silence fell. The sky darkened.

Much later Dan heard Fred locking up. He clumped about his own house as though it was a parade ground. The boys went up to bed at about 11, Fred soon afterwards. Glad Fowler had gone up long before, after clearing away the supper and washing it up.

The only dog in the house seemed, after all, to be Fred's labrador. It probably had a basket in the kitchen or thereabouts; that was a part of the house to stay clear of.

The house was completely silent.

Dan decided it was time to explore. He crept from the new wing of the house into the old part. He found himself in a narrow upstairs corridor. There were three doors, none with any light under them. Softly Dan opened the nearest door. A faint grey rectangle showed an uncurtained open window. It was impossible to see anything else. Dan could hear heavy breathing. There was a smell of cigarette smoke. This was not Glad Fowler's room, then – she likely slept with her window shut anyway. It was not Fred's room, either – Fred smoked a pipe and cigars. One of Fred's boys was sleeping six feet away.

Dan stood listening to the thick breathing. He thought about Fred's boys. One was just seventeen, one two years younger. They went to a grand boarding school. Money had changed their voices, but not their looks. They were big, overweight, moon-faced louts, purse-proud, aggressive. Dan remembered them murdering their ponies when they went hunting as kids in the Pony Club. The probably slept like bolsters after too much food, too much beer, too much television.

The boy in the bed grunted and muttered and moved. Dan froze. The heavy breathing became slow and regular again. Dan shut the door as slow as the moon coming up.

He crept on. Round a corner he saw, through an arch, a broad landing with an overhead light on. He prowled towards the landing, listening intently.

From his knowledge of other big houses, and of the ways of nobs and would-be nobs, he guessed that Fred slept some way away from his sons, in a much bigger room with a dressing-room and its own bathroom. The dressing-room might be a kind of study, an extra office, additional to the main farm office down-stairs. It might have a telephone. It might have a connecting door with the bedroom. The whole suite was probably on this main landing.

Like a mouse, Dan explored the rest of the upstairs of the house, listening all the time for the telephone or for any move-ment. He was sure there would be a telephone call. There had to be.

Sure enough the telephone rang at about 2.30: quite softly: behind one of the doors on the main landing.

Bedsprings creaked. Slippered feet shuffled. A door opened. No doubt a light came on, but Dan couldn't see that from where he was.

Fred Mortimer's voice said, 'Yes? Fine . . . That's champion. Take fifty quid out for yourselves, and put the rest in one o' them tin boxes. Put the box – well, you know the place they call Harley's Farm? . . . Okay, listen close.' Fred gave the caller exact directions to Harley's Farm, burned down during the war and never rebuilt, and where to put the tin box of money.

Fred hung up and went back to bed. Sensible bloke. When

anything happened he was miles away – when his men were collecting money, or poisoning trout, or setting fire to his own barley.

Nobody was going to believe any of this: especially as Fred had suffered damage along with the rest of them, and called in the police. And the more Dan was learning, the less he could go to the police about it, on account of the way he was learning it.

But he was still learning. An important point was, Fred's men didn't know where to go until they were told. They weren't locals, then. There were locals involved – Curly Godden, no doubt kept in line because Fred knew about his shoplifting; Ruby Collis, who'd worked in Fred's betting-shop and maybe pinched a few quid – but these ones tonight were foreign, from Milchester or further off, like the men in the Ighampton housing estate.

Fred had some kind of blackmailing hold over all of them. Was that possible? Were there that many guilty secrets, just in one neighbourhood? How had he found them all out? But he must have done, to keep them all obedient. Because they must know who he was. They must know his name and where he lived, because they rang him up on the telephone.

Meanwhile there was something funny about this telephone. In all the nobs' houses Dan knew, the telephones upstairs were extensions of the telephone downstairs. You had a telephone as it might be in the hall, and an extension by your bed, or in your boudoir, or in your dressing-room. But this telephone had not rung from downstairs. There'd been no noise at all from below. There must be a telephone there – nobody had a telephone upstairs only, that was ridiculous – it was impossible that Fred Mortimer heaved his great bulk all the way upstairs every time his phone rang.

You could switch off the bell of a telephone, some telephones, so as not to wake you up. But who'd switch off the bell of a downstairs telephone when they went upstairs to bed? It didn't happen.

Therefore the telephone upstairs was different – a different line.

Dan very gently turned the knob of the door behind which the telephone had rung. He didn't much fancy going in here. Fred Mortimer was one man he was truly afraid of. But he opened the door and slipped in. The room was small and pitch-dark, full of furniture, smelling of hair-oil and cigars. Dan risked his pencil flash. There was a dressing-table with a lot of big brushes on it, a boot-rack full of Fred's enormous hunting boots, a mahogany wardrobe, a glass-fronted gun-case, fishing rods in another case, some hunting prints. Dan's fingers hovered, itching, over gold-mounted hairbrushes: but he dragged them back. Another time. There was a telephone. Dan blinked his flash at the dial and memorized the number: Milchester 850312. It would have been a Medwell number until recently, but they had closed the local exchange. Great misery that had caused, among nobs who had to get a new set of engraved writing-paper.

There was nothing else besides the telephone to show what Fred used the room for. There wouldn't be. He'd hardly keep files of AgriSecurity business, not just lying around.

The telephone rang, making Dan jump almost out of his shoes. He sped out on to the landing and closed the door softly behind him. He heard the springs, the shuffling slippers, the door of Fred's bedroom.

Fred received a report of another successful payoff.

The telephone rang twice more. Fred sounded pleased. Four payoffs in one night. Might be a thousand, might be much more. Fred and his men were busy. No wonder the Calloways were kept waiting.

By 4.30 Dan had heard all he wanted to. He strolled downstairs and out of the front door. He was tempted to spend the rest of the night in the nice airy spare room in the new wing; but the bare possibility of being found asleep by Fred Mortimer made the hair prickle on the back of his neck.

He was also tempted, violently tempted, to go to Harley's Farm, where four tin boxes of money would be waiting in an old stone trough for Fred Mortimer to collect them. But with reluctance Dan dismissed the idea. Fred's machinery must be working smoothly when Dan inserted his bomb into it. Fred must be unsuspicious. All must seem exactly as usual.

It almost broke Dan's heart to think of all that money in the trough. But Fred had to be dynamited. Until he was, Dan was a fugitive, and no amount of money was any good to him.

Dan headed back to the Priory. It was the place to go. Jake and Ruby would never expect him to come back, after yesterday. Nobody would think of searching for him there. If they did, they'd never find him.

The sky began to pale. Dan hurried, but his mind was busy as he went. What still puzzled him was the why. Fred was rich without any of this. Some of the money was going to Janice, it seemed. Maybe all of it. Some of that was going down to the Yeos, to pamper little Karen. But Fred could look after Janice, and Karen too, without bankrupting himself. What was the secrecy? Why did he need so much extra money, criminal money?

Maybe Janice had suddenly got powerful greedy. Maybe she'd always been greedy. But why did Fred give in? It wasn't like him at all. He could pay his legal obligations without much trouble or shame – why so much on top?

Did Janice have something on Fred, like Fred had on his slaves? What sort of thing? That he got her into bed three or four years ago? That wouldn't earn him any disgrace. More like congratulations and envy. It even fitted his picture of himself as a hearty, rip-roaring, old-fashioned squire.

The Priory kitchen garden gave him food – not a feast, but enough. He hoped his mother had eaten a young roast partridge for dinner. He had a bath in a little warm bathroom under the eaves of the house. The water was cold, but it got him clean and it was wonderfully refreshing. He slept most of the day in a little bed in an attic dormitory.

The whole countryside would be looking for him by now, but there was no reason it should see him. He went by devious ways, early in the evening, to the opulent little house at the edge of the village. The fringes of Priory Wood were noisy with families of magpies – parent birds and their fully-grown young – overdressed, clumsy, chattering, useless, all a bit like Mrs Potter of the Old Mill. Deeper in the woods the jays kept in families too, shouting to each other in their ugly voices, gaudy, conceited, show-off, destructive, a bit like Fred Mortimer. In a hedge Dan found, to his astonishment, a linnet sitting on five blue-white, pink-mottled eggs. He wondered if it was a third brood. The nest was a miracle of comfort, lined with fur and thistledown and a few tiny feathers. He hoped it would be a fine autumn for these dangerously late chicks.

For it was autumn, now, well and truly. The stubble was full of rooks and cushats gleaning after the harvest, and wheatears were gathering on the grasslands to go south. Huge parties of swifts were gathering, too; unlike Dan, they liked company when they travelled. There were plenty of partridges. As soon as these troubles were over, Dan promised himself a new partridge-net as well as a new flask.

Moving like a lizard, Dan crawled to the back of the Galloways' house and slipped into the shed they used as a stable. Old Cherry was still there. She must be on permanent hire to Camilla (as Camilla was on permanent loan to Dan). Cherry was lying down. Dan made himself comfortable sitting on her broad quarters.

He heard voices quacking farewells, a car door slamming, an engine, the crunch of wheels on gravel.

Footsteps approached the shed, and Camilla's fair head leaned in.

133

'Grand evening,' said Dan.

Camilla jumped and gave a little scream.

She said, 'Come and have a drink, sweetie.'

Dan enjoyed Mr Calloway's whisky, and he enjoyed kissing Camilla while he drank it.

After a time Camilla extricated herself from the sofa and lit a cigarette with trembling fingers.

She said, 'The police were here today.'

'Asking for me?'

'Someone told them you worked here.'

'It's no secret.'

'They wanted to know if we'd seen you.'

'You haven't.'

'That's what we said. Mildred's dreadfully shocked. She says she doesn't know what to believe. She told me to lock the doors. So,' Camilla giggled, 'I have. They won't be back till about 11 . . . Here, darling?'

'Yes,' said Dan, who saw no point in further delay.

Half an hour later Camilla lay asprawl on the goatskin hearthrug. The gaps in her suntan made her look as though she was wearing a see-through white bikini.

'When's your husband coming back?' Dan asked suddenly.

'Never, I hope.'

She sighed, sat up, and asked him for a cigarette.

He stood and crossed the room.

Looking at him, she said, 'How do you manage to be so strong when there's so little of you.'

'Clean living,' said Dan.

'By the way,' she said, 'I went and saw your mother.'

'Ah. Thank you. How's she getting on?'

'All right. But I don't think you ought to stay away a minute longer than you have to.'

'I know. It's on my mind all the time. Is she tiring herself out?'

'Of course she is. You knew that without asking.'

'Yes,' admitted Dan sadly.

'I tried to help her a bit. In fact I made her let me carry some potatoes in. But she wasn't at all pleased.'

'She was really,' said Dan. 'She's one of the people who find it hard to say thank you. I don't know why.'

'Independence.'

'Prickly pride.'

'Independence,' said Camilla, 'is the thing I'd like more than anything else in the world. I've never had it, because I've never had any money. It's one of the things I love about you.'

'*I've* never had any money,' objected Dan.

'I know, darling, but *you* don't *need* money. You're complete without it.'

Dan thought about his £1,200. He shrugged and made a face.

'You're more independent than you would be *with* money,' said Camilla. 'You're like a . . . fox? A bird? A badger? But you won't be independent much longer, you know. That's what's worrying your mother. It worries me, too. The police searched your cottage yesterday.'

'I knew they would. They didn't find anything.'

'Yes they did, darling. They found your typewriter.'

'I haven't got a typewriter.'

'In the dog-kennel.'

'Oh,' said Dan. 'And of course they'll match it up . . . What a sneaky trick. Planted that on me, have they? Oh, very sneaky.'

'The police have another reason for looking for you.'

'Yes. And a jury has another reason for convicting me.'

'The police didn't say why they wanted you, when they came here. But we all know why. It's because they think you've been writing letters and extorting money and burning things and blowing up Edwin's greenhouse. But I know you're not doing any of those things.'

'That's nice of you,' said Dan. 'But how do you know?'

'Because I know you. Just a little bit. Enough. I've met your mother and seen your birds and animals. We've made love together.' She looked at him earnestly, her face as solemn as when she had threatened him with a twelve-bore shotgun. She said, 'In a million years you wouldn't poison all those trout. Not in a million years. I'm not very clever or perceptive, and I don't know you very well, but I *do* know *that*.'

Dan smiled. It was not any one of his deliberately effective smiles, but a smile of the purest affection and gratitude.

She smiled back, blushing, and said, 'Have a drink.'

As Dan helped himself to a glass of whisky, the telephone rang.

'Mildred, I bet,' said Camilla, 'ringing up to ask if I've been raped.'

She stood up and crossed the room, a little self-conscious in her nakedness. She picked up the telephone.

'Hullo? . . . Oh. Wait just a moment.'

She covered the mouthpiece with her hand. She whispered, 'It's that man. The same one. About the money.'

'Ah,' murmured Dan. 'That's grand.'

Now, if things worked out right, he could put the match to the touch-paper.

13

Dan took the telephone from Camilla. Standing naked on the lush mushroom carpet he frowned to himself for a moment, remembering the voice he wanted to use, fixing the tone in his mind's ear. It did not have to be a perfect piece of mimicry: he was not dealing with a sensitive listener, an elocution expert.

He said to the telephone, with guarded heartiness, 'Edwin Calloway heah.'

Camilla looked at him with utter amazement. He winked at her.

A calm voice the other end said, 'I hope you has the money for our fee, Mr Calloway, ready by you.'

'Er . . .'

'I hope you has. You'll put it in a water-proof polythene bag. You'll have such a thing for the deep-freeze.'

'I believe so, yes,' said Dan in Mr Calloway's voice.

'You also have, we 'appen to know, an inflatable mattress, like for swimming.'

'Oh yes,' said Dan, not having to act startled.

'You'll blow up the mattress an' fix the money to it in the polythene bag. How you do that is your business. At 4 o'clock tonight, meanin' tomorrow mornin', you'll drop the mattress off the bridge in the village.'

'Yes,' said Dan. 'I'll do that, but it will have to be tomorrow night. I'm sorry. Tonight is impossible.'

'Tomorrow night? Okay, we'll stretch a point. 4 o'clock tomorrow night, meanin' the day after tomorrow morning. No lingerin', no police, no tricks. You know what comes when we gets irritated.'

'Yes,' said Dan.

'Okay, then.'

'Wilco,' said Dan, hanging up.

'Blimey,' said Camilla. 'You sound more like Edwin than Edwin does. Why did you say tomorrow night? Why not tonight, if we've got to pay? It won't make any difference to Edwin. It'll hurt just as much tomorrow. More. He'll have that much longer to brood about it.'

'I have to get myself into position,' said Dan.

'What for?'

'Detonating a bomb.'

'What bomb? I don't understand. Nor will Edwin.'

'Don't tell him.'

'What? But I must tell him! He must put the money in the river! Otherwise this is where bombs will go off. They might kill Cherry. They might kill *me*.'

'No,' said Dan. 'I don't think so.'

Dan considered telling Camilla the whole situation, and his plan for the exposure and destruction of AgriSecurity. But it was too complicated. Anyway, he mistrusted all gentry, all women except his mother (and sometimes even her) and most men. It was safer so.

He said, 'Have you got a local phone book?'

'By the telephone.'

'Oh yes.'

Dan looked up Mortimer and Coxmore. Mortimer, Fred J., had two numbers listed, the second being called 'Farm Office'. Coxmore Farm had that same number listed. Neither of the numbers was Milchester 850312.

Dan said, 'If a man has a number different from the numbers in the book, an extra one –'

'An unlisted number.'

'Ah. It's not a thing I've ever met.'

'I don't think I have either, actually. But lots of people have them. They have an unlisted telephone as well as a listed one. The unlisted number's kept secret. It's frightfully convenient,

138

I wish I could afford it. I'd only give the number to you, so if that telephone rang I'd know it was you ringing.'

'And you can't get that number from the Enquiries?'

'No, that's the whole point of it. You can only get it if the owner tells you. Film stars and celebrities have unlisted numbers, so their friends can ring them up, but they don't get badgered by strangers.'

'Ah. But if I ring Enquiries and ask – What is this number? Whose number is it?'

'They won't tell you. It's just as secret that way round, obviously. I expect they'd say, "This is an unlisted number." '

'So that's how he does it,' said Dan, half aloud. 'I ought to have thought of it long ago. But I never met these unlisted numbers. I am a country mouse, when all's said. But of course a man like Fred, he knows it all . . . So they ring that number, and they don't know who they're talking to . . . He doesn't have to terrorize them – they couldn't squeal if they wanted to . . . And being a Milchester number, instead of the old village one, it might be anywhere for miles round . . .'

Dan dialled Fred Mortimer's unlisted number. Something hissed. A cool female voice answered him, 'Milchester 850312. This is a recorded message. Please leave your name, number, and any message you have, after the third stroke.' There were three pips, then the hiss. After a long pause the cool voice started again, 'Milchester 850312. This is a recorded message.'

The unlisted number was working for AgriSecurity even when Fred was out.

The old Calloways came back soon before midnight. Dan slipped upstairs to Camilla's bedroom; he waited, listening, with the door ajar. The old people sounded sleepy and cross. Dan heard them tell Camilla that the whole conversation at the dinner-party had been about AgriSecurity. There was outspoken criticism of the police, they said. Everyone knew Dan Mallett was in it up to his neck, they said, but the police couldn't find the man.

'He's probably in Ireland by now,' said Mr Calloway, 'laughing at us.'

Dan spent the night in Camilla's bed. It was a mistake. It was a single bed, and she was a restless sleeper. But in the dawn she was wonderful – sleepy and avid, loving and trusting, comforting and comforted.

It was tempting to spend the rest of the day there, but it was not really safe. A woman came in to clean, and wherever she went, Camilla told Dan, Mildred Calloway followed her pointing out things she missed.

Dan left the house quietly, just before 7 in the morning, and went unhurriedly to the Priory. Jake and Ruby were still snoring. Dan peeped into their bedroom. It was sealed up tight and curtained, and smelled like a vixen's earth. Dan went to the attics and caught up on his own sleep.

During wakeful intervals he thought about his plan.

The unlisted telephone number was the key to Fred's whole operation. It was also the key to Dan's whole operation.

Beyond that, it all hung on one thing. The men who were supposed to be picking up Mr Calloway's £500 at 4 in the morning, they had to be strangers to the village. They had to be unaware that Fred Mortimer was their boss, or that Coxmore was their boss's house. From what he'd heard two nights before, Dan thought this was a fair bet. It was the whole point of the unlisted number, that they could call him up without knowing who he was or where he was. When they reported on the telephone, using that number, they'd go where they were told and do what they were told, without knowing who they were doing it to. It all hung on that.

In the early evening Dan went to Coxmore. He was aware, as he skirted the village and crossed the country, that there was a nervy, alert, angry atmosphere everywhere. He saw several police cars. He saw farm workers with shotguns. It would be better to be caught by the police than by some of the farmers.

It was another beautiful evening, and Fred's farmyard was as busy as Milchester market. Fred was shouting to his men like a good-tempered bull. Everything was going well for Fred. Everything seemed normal. He expected to pick up a lot more money tonight. It was a good thing, Dan thought, that he had resisted the temptation to go to Harley's Farm and collect those tin boxes. All the same, it was heartbreaking.

Dan crept round to the kitchen door, and slipped in when Glad Fowler's back was turned. He would have liked a long talk to Glad. She looked like a shrivelled old weasel, but she was sharp enough. She might be able to answer some of the most puzzling questions in Dan's mind, such as why Fred needed so much extra money all of a sudden, and what, if anything, Janice had on him, and why he was so ashamed of little Karen. But a long talk to Glad would have to wait. To be spotted by her now would be suicide.

Dan crept up the back stairs. His heart thumped with fright at being where he was. He was not ashamed of being scared of Fred Mortimer. He holed up in the gracious spare bedroom, not really relaxing until he heard Fred clump round the house locking the doors and windows.

Another nap would have been a good idea, but Dan was too tense to sleep.

His plan went round and round in his mind. Fred's men, waiting by the river downstream from the bridge, would eventually ring the unlisted number and report that no mattress had been dropped. They would be sent at once on a mission of punishment. Hopefully, they would not know where they were being sent. They would follow Fred's orders blindly. The other crucial point was timing. How long would they wait before deciding the mattress wasn't in the river? How long would they take to get to a telephone? If Fred left the house, how quickly would he leave? How fast would he drive in his Bentley? How long would he stay, when he got where he was going? How fast would he drive back? Above all, what time would he get back?

Dan calculated speeds and distances in his mind until the figures whirled like chaff in a thresher.

After midnight the house was completely silent. It was dark except for the dim light over the landing.

At 2 o'clock Dan went softly down the main stairs. Using his pencil flash, he looked first for a telephone. He found one in a big sitting-room. The number on the dial was the one printed in the telephone book.

Then Dan looked for Fred's whisky, which he found in the sideboard in the baronial dining-room. It was better than Mr Calloway's whisky.

The telephone upstairs purred at 2.30 and 3 and 3.30. The conversations were brief. Everything was going smoothly for AgriSecurity. Fred was still pulling in the money.

Four o'clock. The moment Mr Calloway's inflated mattress ought to be plumping into the water below the bridge. Dan waited as long as he dared – till five past four, ten past. He dared wait no longer after that, in case Fred's men rang from the river. At 4.11 he crept into the sitting-room, closed the door, picked up the telephone. He dialled 850312, the unlisted number of the telephone upstairs.

He heard, faintly, the telephone ringing above him. He heard movements.

Fred's voice on the telephone said, 'Yes?'

Dan had been remembering a grey, pain-filled face, a man pinned to a chair in front of a TV set, a bored man with nothing to do except feel sorry for himself. His mind's ear remembered, clearly enough, the voice that went with the face.

Dan said, in the glum voice he remembered. 'Mr Mortimer? This is Bob Yeo here – '

'What? How in hell d'you know this number?'

'Janice give it.'

'How in hell did she know it?'

'I dunno, Mr Mortimer. She's 'ere, just arrived in a car. She give me the number an' ask me to ring you.'

'All right, put her on.'

'No, she say she won't talk to you, Mr Mortimer. She just give a message.'

'Ah, Christ. Okay, what is the message?'

What was the message? Everything pointed to the fact that Janice had something on Fred: but what it was Dan had no glimmerings of a idea. It might involve little Karen. Beyond that, Dan was in the dark.

Dan made a wild stab at getting Fred rattled. He said, 'Janice say she's goin' to the police, Mr Mortimer.'

'Why?'

Why? Dan said, 'I dunno. Mr Mortimer. Janice say *you'll* know, sure enough . . . Eh? . . . Janice say, she's going to the police an' the newspapers.'

'Ah, Christ. Okay, tell her to come over here.'

'She can't. We don't have no car.'

'She *came* in a car '

'The bloke drops her an' goes off.'

'Tell her to take a taxi in the morning. I'll pay for the bleeding thing.'

'I'll ask . . . No, Mr Mortimer. Janice say, she's goin' to the police an' the newspapers in the mornin'.'

'Bloody hell!' Fred's voice upstairs was beginning to sound very angry. It crackled out of the telephone into Dan's ear.

Dan said, making another stab in the semi-darkness, 'We didn't know you was Karen's dad, Mr Mortimer.'

'Who says I am?'

'Janice.'

'What does the bitch want?' shouted Fred.

'Maybe,' said Dan hopefully, 'maybe if you was to come over, Mr Mortimer . . .'

'Ah, Christ. Okay. In the morning.'

'Janice say, first thing in the mornin' she's goin' to the police an' the newspapers.'

'But I can't come now!'

'Well, then,' said Dan, beginning to feel a certain desperation, 'Janice say, she's goin' to – '

'Is it money she wants? More money? Christ, how much does she need?'

'I dunno nothin' about that, Mr Mortimer. Janice 'asn't said nothin' about that.'

'Ah, Christ. Okay, I'll come.'

Dan was careful to hang up at the same moment as Fred hung up, so no telltale *ping* went up to Fred through the ceiling.

Fred was immediately crashing about upstairs, and in a very few minutes thumping down the stairs and unlocking the front door. A car started. Headlights blazed. Fred's Bentley purred away towards Ighampton.

Dan wondered what on earth Fred had made of the conversation. What did he think Janice was going to tell the police and the newspapers in the morning? What newspapers? The *Milchester Argus*? What was he frightened of? Anyway, it was serious enough to get him out of his house and into his car at 4.30 in the morning.

Dan ran upstairs and into Fred's dressing-room. He wondered if Fred had woken up his sons. He thought it unlikely. He also thought the sons would have been told not to notice or remember anything they heard at night – not to have any idea, in the morning, that their father had ever left his bed.

Dan found that Fred had connected the answering device to the unlisted telephone. The recorder was supposed to tell him, when he got back from Ighampton, that his men had got Mr Calloway's money safe. Dan was familiar with the mechanism. The bank had never used such a thing, but many of its clients had. He disconnected it. The men must ring any minute, if they hadn't already rung.

He waited, tense, in the darkness of Fred's opulent dressing-room. He waited for seven crawling minutes. A brass clock ticked softly on the mantelpiece. There was no other sound except the beating of Dan's heart.

The telephone rang. He let it ring four times, as though he was getting himself out of bed and into the dressing-room. It required iron self-control, to keep from grabbing it at once. He picked it up.

In Fred Mortimer's voice he said, 'Yes?'

A voice said, 'Another clever bastard.'

'No mattress?'

'Not a sign.'

'That's a shame,' said Dan in Fred's voice, and in words he had heard Fred use. 'You and your mate then – '

'An' a few cans of gas?'

'Not half. You don't know where to go?'

'Same place where we put the fireworks in the greenhouse?'

'No,' said Dan. 'Not this time. Listen careful.'

He gave the caller exact directions to Coxmore Farm; he gave him orders about what to do when he got there.

14

Dan went softly downstairs and out.

The villains had not talked from a call-box, so they had the use of a private telephone in or very near the village. Curly Godden's? Did he have a telephone? Anyway there was nothing to stop them getting here inside five minutes. Fred had to get to Ighampton, knock up the sleeping Yeos, sort out a total misunderstanding, and then come back. By the time he got back the villains should have made a useful start.

Within seconds of talking to the Yeos, Fred would know he'd been tricked. He'd think at first it was them, maybe under someone's orders. But eventually he'd realize that they didn't know he was Karen's father, didn't know his unlisted number, weren't in touch with Janice. Obviously the point of the call had been to get him out of the way for half an hour or so. He'd be thinking furiously as he roared back from Ighampton in his enormous car: he'd be wondering why anyone wanted him out of the way. A simple burglar? How would a simple burglar know his unlisted telephone number? Because it was one of his own villains? That possibility must occur to him, considering the kind of men he employed. The thought would make him very angry indeed. Who else besides a thief would want him out of his house? A sleuth, wanting to search the place for evidence? That thought would occur to Fred, too. It would annoy him, but it wouldn't bother him much, because there was nothing incriminating in the house. The whole County police could take Coxmore Farm to bits without finding anything to link Fred to AgriSecurity. Even the typewriter which had written the threatening letters had been planted on Dan.

Coxmore Farm was clean, except for one absolutely damning thing, which the police wouldn't know when they saw it. The telephone with the unlisted number.

Fred would think fast and in the right directions, because he was a clever man. He'd think: whoever pulled the trick knew about Janice and Karen and the Yeos. Such as who? Such as Dan. Fred knew Dan knew about the Yeos – he had been to see them. Fred would see Dan's footprints all over tonight's frolic. If he did see them, he'd be almost senseless with rage, especially remembering he'd had Dan helpless in a ditch with a pitchfork skewering his belly.

Dan was all for Fred Mortimer being senseless with rage, as long as he didn't have to meet him himself. That would be a very bad idea. It was another good reason for getting clear away from the house.

Thirty yards from the sleeping farm, Dan stood on a wall. He listened intently for one of two car engines. One was due now: it was overdue: and Dan heard it, a long way away on the main road. It approached, still far away but clearly audible in the quiet night. It was not Fred's Bentley but a smaller car. Dan saw the glow of the headlights, although the headlights themselves were hidden by a rise of ground.

The glow disappeared. But the engine was still audible, going slow and quiet. They were crawling along with sidelights on. Dan realized that, like good boys, they were putting the car where he'd told them to, on a side-track off Fred's main drive which led to a different road. They'd walk bold as brass up the main drive to the house and farmyard, carrying their petrol cans, safe from meeting anybody at this time of night. They'd been told – Dan had told them – that everybody was asleep and there was no watchdog outside.

Dan heard them coming up the drive, two of them, although they were trying to move quietly.

He himself went briskly across two fields to where their car was. He listened, as he went, for Fred's Bentley. He hoped Fred wouldn't be too soon, or too late either.

He got to the parked car; he prowled round it, making sure they had not left a third man with the car. It was unattended and unlocked. He opened the bonnet, used his pencil flash cautiously, and unclipped the distributor head. It was a good car, a Rover; Dan was sure it was stolen.

No doubt the owner could afford a new distributor head. Dan threw it far into a field of young kale.

He saw the fire as he turned.

They started on the Swiss-roll bales and the straw-ricks. The hay in the Dutch barn followed, the farm buildings, the combine and tractors, the cars, the milking-shed.

Dan, who had made a point of searching, knew there were no stalled animals near the farmhouse. Fred's hunters were not yet up from grass, and he wouldn't have pigs or bullocks within range of his windows.

Noise and glare would wake up even Fred's heavy-sleeping sons. They'd ring the fire-brigade: perhaps the police too. Old Glad might wake up first, but it was hard to picture her using a telephone. The police would come anyway, because the fire-station would report the fire to them. There must be an arrangement like that, since AgriSecurity started. The fire-engine would have to come from Milchester. It might just about tie with Fred.

Dan started back, unhurriedly, towards the inferno of the farmyard. He felt the heat and was dazzled by the glare when he was still quite a long way off. He decided he was near enough. It was a great sight, and surpassed his best hopes. Straw, hay, thatch, planking and beams were as dry as tinder after the long fine spell. There were satisfactory explosions from the fuel-tanks of the tractors and cars. Dan was a little awed at what he had done – at the spectacle he had created with a brief telephone call in a borrowed voice.

Then the new part of the house caught. It was well away from the farmyard; there was no reason it should have caught as it did, with a sudden pillar of flame up one side. Dan guessed the AgriSecurity men had found themselves with a gallon of petrol to spare. They hadn't wanted to waste it, nor carry it back to their car. They'd exceeded instructions.

It was still possible for the people inside, in the old part of the house, to come out safely, if they were awake and not delirious with terror. Dan was a little worried about old Glad: but after a moment he was reassured. He heard her screams from the garden. She was safe. There was no reason for her to scream. But it was understandable. The size and noise of the fire was enough to make anybody scream. The boys were out, too. They were stampeding round the garden like bullocks with the gadfly. Their voices promised to be as bull-like as Fred's own. A bark laid Dan's final worry. Blinker was safe. Blinker was not a dog Dan had much reason to love, but he did not want the creature roasted alive.

Dan guessed the AgriSecurity men were already back at their car. If they had any sense they'd abandon it the moment they failed to start it. But Dan betted they wouldn't do that. They'd want to get clear away, far away, quick, before police or fireman arrived; and they wouldn't want to walk home to Milchester. The car had been working perfectly a few minutes before: it *must* start – it was overchoked, or there was an airlock – that's what they'd tell each other. They'd keep the self-starter churning until the battery began to run low. It would never occur to them anyone had fiddled with the car, not for a long time.

More headlights glared on the road, but the engine was inaudible over the tremendous noise of the fire. The beams swung into Fred's drive. It was impossible to see the vehicle behind them. Whatever it was, it came very fast up the drive, insanely fast. Dan thought it was Fred's Bentley.

It was.

It screeched to a halt, the screech audible from where Dan stood even over the noise of the fire. Fred stopped at a safe distance from the fire: it did not occur to him, perhaps, that he was blocking his own drive. He was probably past rational thought – first enraged by the wild-goose chase to Ighampton, then by what he guessed was the cause of that, and now by what he saw was the result of it. Dan had seen him almost berserk, roaring and charging with a pitchfork. A pitchfork hadn't helped him then, and it wouldn't help him now.

Shouts greeted Fred when Glad and the boys became aware of him. Maybe they were trying to tell him what had happened. But they didn't know what had happened, and he was in no mood to listen to anyone.

The situation at the farmhouse would change very little in the next few minutes, Dan thought, except that the house itself would get smaller; he thought it was time to visit the men with the disabled car. He had an idea as he went, and equipped himself with a four-foot stick out of a hedgerow.

The men were still churning the starting-motor, but it sounded tired.

'You been an' flattened the battery,' said one, his voice almost a wail of despair.

'It were workin' perfect,' mumbled the other. 'It were workin' perfect.'

He tried the starter again. It turned over sluggishly.

Until the battery was completely flat they'd go on trying. It was silly but it was human nature. The car *had* been working perfectly.

Dan saw more headlights. Here, well away from the fire, he could hear the clang and wail of public servants. A fire-engine roared up the drive, with two cars behind and another fire-engine behind them. But the convoy screeched to a halt well back from the farm because Fred's Bentley was blocking the drive.

'Christ,' moaned one of the men in the car.

They scrambled out and started to stumble away up the side-track.

Dan ran to the car, switched on the headlights, and jammed his stick between the horn-button and the back of the driver's seat. The battery might be failing with the starter-motor, but it was still well up to headlights and horn.

The two men were impaled by the brilliant undipped headlights. One was the big buck-toothed man whom Dan had previously seen in a crash-helmet; the other was a tall, thin, sick-looking fellow with a small moustache and greasy grey hair. They both scrambled out of the track and began to run across a field. Behind, in the main drive, a car wailed, turned, and began to aproach at speed. Long before it arrived, Dan was clear and hidden; without dogs the police had no hope of finding him, even if they had known to look for him. But they found the other two quite quickly. The two had stayed together, which was foolish; perhaps neither trusted the other; perhaps both were afraid to be alone. The big man's speed and grace of movement seemed to have deserted him; they seemed to be unmanned by their car not starting. They offered no resistance. They loudly denied having any connection with any fire. They said they had spotted the fire and come to see if they could help. Their car had stalled. This was all they said, but they said it again and again. They were put in the police car and taken up towards the house. Their car's horn continued to blare until a policeman took Dan's stick away.

Dan trotted back towards the farm. He was interested to see the next scene, which he thought would be decisive.

Fred's car had been moved and the fire-engines were already jetting water into the farmhouse. They were too late to do anything to save the farm buildings, vehicles or crops, and they could not do much for the new, wood-and-glass part of the house. The best they could hope for was to save the old part of the house, and they seemed to be succeeding.

The foxy Superintendent was there, trying to get sense out of Fred Mortimer. He was not having much luck with Fred, who was like a man possessed, beside himself, violently angry and shaken by violent grief.

The two firebugs, buck-teeth and moustache, were led towards a patch lit like a TV studio by police spotlights. Fred suddenly saw them as they came into the full glare of the lights. This was the moment Dan had been looking forward to – the moment which had become inevitable when he made the call to Fred and took the call from the others. Fred's mouth dropped open. He knew who the men were and what they had just done. He shouted something completely incoherent — it might have been in a foreign language — and threw his arms out as though he was being crucified. Then he rushed at them. They both squealed and tried to duck behind the policemen who had arrested them. They were much more frightened of this furious giant than they were of anything else. They were quite right to be. The police tried to restrain Fred. He tossed them aside like dolls. At one point, it seemed to Dan, there were three policemen holding each of Fred's legs and three holding each of his arms. He shook them all off and tried to rush at the men he recognized. It made Dan think of a bullfight, which he had never seen but clearly imagined. Behind, like a mad backdrop to the spotlit foreground scene, flames still towered from the gutted barns, and, silhouetted against the glare, firemen on ladders hosed water into the house.

Suddenly Fred stopped, in the middle of his charge. He looked round, his mouth still open. Dan realized he was looking for a weapon. There was nothing obvious to hand, no club or scythe or axe, no slasher or pitchfork or gun.

Fred turned and ran back towards the fire. Policemen ran after him. He knocked a fireman aside and ran into the end of the old barn. He seemed oblivious of the belching smoke and the flames licking up the walls and consuming the roof above him. It seemed absolutely certain that the roof would collapse on him.

It did.

First a single beam, still somehow attached at one end, came scything down, blazing, and at last fell: and then the whole roof followed. The fire blazed up from the ground, celebrating this new fuel. Fred was somewhere in the middle of it all. Firemen approached with ideas of rescue, only to back away from the intense heat, the renewed fury of flames and belching of smoke.

Neither of the boys was anywhere near the barn when it happened. This was a relief to everyone. A middle-aged policeman went to find them.

Old Glad Fowler was there watching. She screamed when her master ran into the barn, but she was silent when the roof fell down. It was as though all her screaming was spent. She had no more screams to give.

No one else said much. There was little to say. Dawn came. The fire was under control – it had destroyed the farm buildings completely, damaged part of the farmhouse severely, not much damaged the old house, the big downstairs rooms, the main staircase and landing, Fred's upstairs suite. The rooms were soaked and smoke-blackened but they were still there. The firemen and the remaining policemen were exhausted, unshaven, filthy.

Dan realized that a silent crowd had collected, somehow, during the night. It included Curly Godden, Jake and Ruby Collis, a few others from the village and the nearer cottages and farms. Dan allowed it to include himself, as though he too had wandered up from somewhere to see the show. He was seen; a cry rose; he was arrested and brought to the Superintendent, who was sitting, looking utterly exhausted, on the bonnet of a police car.

'I've been looking for you,' said the Superintendent.

'Ay,' said Dan meekly. 'But I thought it was best not to bother you, when you were bothered by more important things. Have you spoken to those blokes, sir, since their boss got burned?'

'No. Why?'

'I think they'll do a sight more talking, now Fred isn't there to threaten. Like – hum – how did they get their orders? What telephone number did they ring? Why did they do exactly what he told them?'

The Superintendent looked at Dan, frowning, for a long time. He seemed too tired to get up off the bonnet of the car. Dan himself suddenly felt too tired to stand a moment longer; he subsided to the dew-wet ground and squatted by the wheel of the police car.

Dan thought the Superintendent would put off asking any more questions of anybody until he had had some rest: but the Superintendent climbed at last heavily off the car. He went over to buck-teeth and moustache, who were sitting back-to-back, infinitely dejected, with a policeman standing over them.

The Superintendent talked to the men for a long time. Then he sent one of his own men into the house. The firemen were against this, but he said it was necessary. He said he would go in himself, but before he could do so his man went in, carefully, and up the main stairs.

The policeman came out after a few minutes, coughing a little from the smoke. He had written something down on a piece of paper, which he gave to the Superintendent.

The Superintendent nodded. He sent the policeman to make enquiries on the telephone of a police car. Dan heard the policeman asking to be put through to the Night Supervisor on the Milchester telephone exchange. Then he heard questions about an unlisted number.

The Superintendent did not look at Dan or talk to him. Dan got the impression he was still under arrest, but this was not absolutely clear. The Superintendent was talking, some way off, to Fred's sons. The boys seemed to be taking it all pretty well.

Dan heaved himself to his feet. The policemen ignored him. He went and squatted down beside old Glad Fowler, who was looking a bit dizzy, and wearing an amazing dressing-gown like the cover of an ancient sofa.

Dan said, 'You must ha' known Fred better'n anybody.'

'Ay. A-knowed about un.'

'About Janice?'

'A-knowed about Janice.'

'Why did Fred all of a sudden start to send such a lot of money to Janice?'

'She arst.'

'An' Fred just sent it, the moment she asked?'

' 'Ad t'send un.'

'Why?'

'She say she telt, else.'

'She said she'd tell? Tell what, Glad?'

' 'Bout Fred an' her.'

'The baby?'

'Ay.'

'Fred.'

'Fred was that ashamed? That ashamed of one little love-child?'

'Ah, but 'oo were her mother?'

'The child's mother? Janice, of course.'

'Ah, but 'oo were *her* mother?'

'Janice's mother? I never knew. Does it matter?'

'She were called Gwennie,' said old Glad. 'Swate pretty lass. Cam' a-worken up-along yere in the war. Land-girl, they called un.'

'Workin' here? At Coxmore?'

'Ay, an't a-tellen ye?'

'So, Gwennie the land-girl was Janice's ma. So?'

'Ay, but 'oo were Janice's pa?'

'God Almighty,' said Dan. 'He had Gwennie when Gwennie worked here . . . and then when Janice came and worked here . . . Fred done his own daughter unbeknownst?'

'Unbeknownst to she,' said old Glad.

'Fred knew who Janice was?'

'A-dunno?' she admitted. 'But *I* knowed.'

'How?'

'Gwennie wrote t'tell I, for t'kip a eye on Janice, when Janice cam' yere t'be seckyterry.'

'You didn't keep much of an eye.'

'Ay. A-likes a-watchen.'

'Through keyholes?'

'A-seed what a-seed.'

'Why didn't you tell Janice what she was doing?'

'A-dursen stand i' the way o' Fred's lust.'

'How did Janice get to hear who her father was?'

'A-telled her.'

'*You* told Janice?'

'Ay.'

'You told her Fred was her own pa as well as Karen's pa?'

'Ay.'

'When?'

'Jist two-three month agone. She cam' t'see Karen, an' she cam' t'see Fred, an' a-telled her.'

'That do explain everything,' murmured Dan. 'Why it started when it started. Why Fred needed the money. Why he sent everything Janice asked for. Why the poor little kid's lacking . . . Glad – *why* d'you tell Janice?'

' 'Cause,' said old Glad, 'a-bent had no amusemen' for fifty year.'

Dan sat back on his haunches, stupefied. It occurred to him that Glad's screams in the night were screams of pure delight at the show, of joy in the mischief she had made.

'I might,' said the Superintendent, 'never have paid attention to the different number on that telephone in the upstairs room.'

'Ay,' said Dan guardedly.

'As you realize, that number completely establishes Mortimer's guilt. Now – you asked why these hoodlums did exactly what he told them, without daring to blackmail him. Well, we'll probably never know how he controlled all of them, because we'll never find all of them, but those two are probably representative.'

'Eh?' said Dan.

'Much like most of the rest. One of those two owed more money than he could pay to the betting-shop in Milchester.'

'Simple as that?'

'With one kind of betting-shop owner, as simple as that.'

'Did Fred still own the betting-shop?'

'A majority share, yes.'

'I s'pose that's where he met those lovely people he hired?'

'No, he didn't meet them. He had a look at them through a spy-hole, I imagine, got their names, found out about them, eavesdropped on their chat. All very easy if you own the shop. And a betting-shop is on the fringe of racing, the fringe of crime. It's the number one meeting-place of layabouts, it's a perfect recruiting station. Especially if the blokes got into debt.'

'He saw them, they never saw him?'

'That's right. That's the other reason they didn't try to blackmail him. They didn't know who he was.'

Dan nodded. 'That's what they told me. I didn't believe it, 'cause I didn't think about an unlisted telephone . . . I thought you thought the villain was me.'

'I had very grave suspicions about you, Mallett. I still have. But I don't think you had anything to do with AgriSecurity.'

'Why not?'

'When we found that typewriter in your dog-kennel, I knew you'd never used it '

'Was it the typewriter that wrote the letters?'

'Oh yes.'

'Why couldn't I ha' used it?'

'Because you would have hidden it better.'

'Oh.'

'Obvious, isn't it? *You* hide an incriminating typewriter as unskilfully as that? Never. You'd do something very different. I don't know where you'd put it, but I don't suppose we'd find it.'

'Oh,' said Dan. 'Did Fred write all those letters himself?'

'Oh no. His sons wrote them. They're having a very expensive education, you know.'

'Those boys? God Almighty.'

'They were terrified of their father. The moment they knew he was well and truly dead, they sang like linnets. I don't mean they're glad he's dead, exactly. But it certainly changes their attitude to AgriSecurity. I don't suppose we shall take action against them. All they did was write letters, and they were clearly terrorized into that. Now,' said the Superintendent, 'there are one or two things I would like to know from you.'

'Ay,' said Dan, alert, wondering what was coming.

'Those two sweethearts who've just been taken away, they admit to starting the fire. They swear they were told to come here and burn the farmyard down, *by* the voice they knew, *on* the telephone they knew.'

'Amazin',' said Dan.

'You'd have no idea how that happened?'

'I guess,' said Dan, 'Fred Mortimer wanted the insurance money.'

'That wasn't the impression I received,' said the Superintendent, 'when he tried to kill his own bully-boys.'

'Then 'e was barmy.'

'The AgriSecurity operation, all in all, was *not* the work of a man who was, er, barmy.'

'*Went* barmy, just tonight.'

'Yes? I suppose we must accept that it *was* Mortimer who gave those extraordinary instructions on the telephone. I suppose we shall never know why he gave them. One of the great and permanently insoluble mysteries, the *Marie Celeste* of our time.'

'Ay,' said Dan.

'There's another question I think you *can* answer.'

'Ay?' said Dan, his caution undiminished.

'How did you know Fred Mortimer was controlling AgriSecurity?'

'That was simple,' said Dan modestly. 'That was obvious.'

'Enlighten me.'

'Eh?'

'How *did* you know?'

'I knew Fred was a greedy bastard. I didn't know he'd poison trout an' such, but I knew he was a greedy bastard. So I knew there was something fishy when I saw that field o' barley.'

'What was fishy about it?'

'Headlands.'

'Unploughed strips at the sides of the fields?'

'Ay. Waste o' ground.'

'You suspected something fishy about Mortimer the moment you saw unploughed headlands on that particular field?'

'Ay. Anybody would.'

'Not quite anybody, perhaps . . . You do mean the field that was burned?'

'Ay. Nice tidy fire, hardly touched a twig o' the trees.'

'I understand. You realized that Mortimer had carefully prepared himself for just such a fire, to be started by his own men, by leaving those headlands. He sent a letter to himself, showed it to us, and then, sure enough, had his barley burned. It all put him completely beyond suspicion, even if there'd been any grounds for suspecting him . . . And he was claiming the insurance . . . And the fire did no unforeseen damage, because of his precaution with the headlands. *Ergo*, AgriSecurity had to be Mortimer, and the headlands gave him away.'

'About like that,' agreed Dan.

The Superintendent stood frowning for a long minute. Then he said, 'AgriSecurity began operations about a month ago.'

'Ay.'

'As you know everything else, I suppose you know why?'

'Ay. Fred needed a lot of money sudden.'

'This was a new need, which suddenly declared itself?'

'Ay.'

'A need he could not have predicted?'

'No.'

'What was the need?'

'He was being blackmailed,' said Dan, slipping unconsciously into his banker's voice, 'by an ex-mistress, the mother of his bastard, who was also his own daughter.'

'Ah. Even I might pay blackmail, if I found myself in quite such an unsavoury position . . . When did the ex-mistress start putting the squeeze on him?'

'She knew the truth herself two or three months ago.'

'So it was then, or soon afterwards, that Mortimer's need for money declared itself?'

'Yes.'

'Early May? Early June?'

'Thereabouts.'

'Not before?'

'Oh no.'

'He left broad headlands in that field of barley which he himself burned.'

'Yes.'

'When was that field ploughed?'

'A year back,' said Dan.

Over the next few seconds he saw, rushing at him, all the implications.

The Superintendent said, 'There may have been a thousand reasons why Fred Mortimer left headlands in the barley field. But AgriSecurity wasn't one of them.'

'No,' agreed Dan.

'You guessed right, but your reasons could hardly have been more wrong.'

'It's lucky,' said Dan sententiously, 'we have the police force.'

THE PERENNIAL LIBRARY MYSTERY SERIES

Delano Ames

CORPSE DIPLOMATIQUE   P 637, $2.84
"Sprightly and intelligent."

— *New York Herald Tribune Book Review*

FOR OLD CRIME'S SAKE   P 629, $2.84

MURDER, MAESTRO, PLEASE   P 630, $2.84
"If there is a more engaging couple in modern fiction than Jane and
Dagobert Brown, we have not met them."   — *Scotsman*

HE SHALL HAVE MURDER   P 638, $2.84
"Combines the merit of both the English and American schools in the
new mystery. It's as breezy as the best of the American ones, and has
the sophistication and wit of any top-notch Britisher."

— *New York Herald Tribune Book Review*

E. C. Bentley

TRENT'S LAST CASE   P 440, $2.50
"One of the three best detective stories ever written."

— Agatha Christie

TRENT'S OWN CASE   P 516, $2.25
"I won't waste time saying that the plot is sound and the detection
satisfying. Trent has not altered a scrap and reappears with all his old
humor and charm."   — Dorothy L. Sayers

Gavin Black

A DRAGON FOR CHRISTMAS   P 473, $1.95
"Potent excitement!"   — *New York Herald Tribune*

THE EYES AROUND ME   P 485, $1.95
"I stayed up until all hours last night reading *The Eyes Around Me*,
which is something I do not do very often, but I was so intrigued by the
ingeniousness of Mr. Black's plotting and the witty way in which he spins
his mystery. I can only say that I enjoyed the book enormously."

— F. van Wyck Mason

YOU WANT TO DIE, JOHNNY?   P 472, $1.95
"Gavin Black doesn't just develop a pressure plot in suspense, he adds
uninfected wit, character, charm, and sharp knowledge of the Far East
to make rereading as keen as the first race-through."   — *Book Week*

Nicholas Blake

THE CORPSE IN THE SNOWMAN P 427, $1
"If there is a distinction between the novel and the detective story (whi
we do not admit), then this book deserves a high place in both cate
ries." —*The New York Tim*

THE DREADFUL HOLLOW P 493, $1.
"Pace unhurried, characters excellent, reasoning solid."
—*San Francisco Chroni*

END OF CHAPTER P 397, $1.
". . . admirably solid . . . an adroit formal detective puzzle backed
by firm characterization and a knowing picture of London publishin
—*The New York Tim*

HEAD OF A TRAVELER P 398, $2.
"Another grade A detective story of the right old jigsaw persuasion
—*New York Herald Tribune Book Revi*

MINUTE FOR MURDER P 419, $1.
"An outstanding mystery novel. Mr. Blake's writing is a delight
itself." —*The New York Tim*

THE MORNING AFTER DEATH P 520, $1.
"One of Blake's best." —*Rex Warr*

A PENKNIFE IN MY HEART P 521, $2.
"Style brilliant . . . and suspenseful." —*San Francisco Chroni*

THE PRIVATE WOUND P 531, $2.
[Blake's] best novel in a dozen years . . . . An intensely penetrating stu
of sexual passion. . . . A powerful story of murder and its aftermath
—Anthony Boucher, *The New York Tim*

A QUESTION OF PROOF P 494, $1.
"The characters in this story are unusually well drawn, and the suspen
is well sustained." —*The New York Tim*

THE SAD VARIETY P 495, $2.
"It is a stunner. I read it instead of eating, instead of sleeping."
—Dorothy Salisbury Da

THERE'S TROUBLE BREWING P 569, $3.
"Nigel Strangeways is a puzzling mixture of simplicity and penetratic
but all the more real for that." —*The Times Literary Suppleme*

Nicholas Blake (cont'd)

THOU SHELL OF DEATH   P 428, $1.95
"It has all the virtues of culture, intelligence and sensibility that the most exacting connoisseur could ask of detective fiction."
                    —*The Times* [London] *Literary Supplement*

THE WIDOW'S CRUISE   P 399, $2.25
"A stirring suspense. . . . The thrilling tale leaves nothing to be desired."
                    —*Springfield Republican*

THE WORM OF DEATH   P 400, $2.25
"It [The Worm of Death] is one of Blake's very best—and his best is better than almost anyone's."
                    —Louis Untermeyer

John & Emery Bonett

A BANNER FOR PEGASUS   P 554, $2.40
"A gem! Beautifully plotted and set. . . . Not only is the murder adroit and deserved, and the detection competent, but the love story is charming."
                    —Jacques Barzun and Wendell Hertig Taylor

DEAD LION   P 563, $2.40
"A clever plot, authentic background and interesting characters highly recommended this one."
                    —*New Republic*

Christianna Brand

GREEN FOR DANGER   P 551, $2.50
"You have to reach for the greatest of Great Names (Christie, Carr, Queen . . .) to find Brand's rivals in the devious subtleties of the trade."
                    —Anthony Boucher

TOUR DE FORCE   P 572, $2.40
"Complete with traps for the over-ingenious, a double-reverse surprise ending and a key clue planted so fairly and obviously that you completely overlook it. If that's your idea of perfect entertainment, then seize at once upon *Tour de Force.*"   —Anthony Boucher, *The New York Times*

James Byrom

OR BE HE DEAD   P 585, $2.84
"A very original tale . . . Well written and steadily entertaining."
    —Jacques Barzun & Wendell Hertig Taylor, *A Catalogue of Crime*

Henry Calvin

IT'S DIFFERENT ABROAD P 640, $2.84

"What is remarkable and delightful, Mr. Calvin imparts a flavor of satire to what he renovates and compels us to take straight."

—Jacques Barzun

Marjorie Carleton

VANISHED P 559, $2.40

"Exceptional . . . a minor triumph."

—Jacques Barzun and Wendell Hertig Taylor, *A Catalogue of Crime*

George Harmon Coxe

MURDER WITH PICTURES P 527, $2.25

"[Coxe] has hit the bull's-eye with his first shot."

—*The New York Times*

Edmund Crispin

BURIED FOR PLEASURE P 506, $2.50

"Absolute and unalloyed delight."

—Anthony Boucher, *The New York Times*

Lionel Davidson

THE MENORAH MEN P 592, $2.84

"Of his fellow thriller writers, only John Le Carré shows the same instinct for the viscera." —*Chicago Tribune*

NIGHT OF WENCESLAS P 595, $2.84

"A most ingenious thriller, so enriched with style, wit, and a sense of serious comedy that it all but transcends its kind."

—*The New Yorker*

THE ROSE OF TIBET P 593, $2.84

"I hadn't realized how much I missed the genuine Adventure story . . . until I read *The Rose of Tibet*." —Graham Greene

D. M. Devine

MY BROTHER'S KILLER P 558, $2.40

"A most enjoyable crime story which I enjoyed reading down to the last moment." —Agatha Christie

Kenneth Fearing

THE BIG CLOCK P 500, $1.95

"It will be some time before chill-hungry clients meet again so rare a compound of irony, satire, and icy-fingered narrative. *The Big Clock* is . . . a psychothriller you won't put down." —*Weekly Book Review*

Andrew Garve

THE ASHES OF LODA P 430, $1.50

"Garve . . . embellishes a fine fast adventure story with a more credible picture of the U.S.S.R. than is offered in most thrillers."
—*The New York Times Book Review*

THE CUCKOO LINE AFFAIR P 451, $1.95

". . . an agreeable and ingenious piece of work." —*The New Yorker*

A HERO FOR LEANDA P 429, $1.50

"One can trust Mr. Garve to put a fresh twist to any situation, and the ending is really a lovely surprise." —*The Manchester Guardian*

MURDER THROUGH THE LOOKING GLASS P 449, $1.95

". . . refreshingly out-of-the-way and enjoyable . . . highly recommended to all comers." —*Saturday Review*

NO TEARS FOR HILDA P 441, $1.95

"It starts fine and finishes finer. I got behind on breathing watching Max get not only his man but his woman, too." —Rex Stout

THE RIDDLE OF SAMSON P 450, $1.95

"The story is an excellent one, the people are quite likable, and the writing is superior." —*Springfield Republican*

Michael Gilbert

BLOOD AND JUDGMENT P 446, $1.95

"Gilbert readers need scarcely be told that the characters all come alive at first sight, and that his surpassing talent for narration enhances any plot. . . . Don't miss." —*San Francisco Chronicle*

THE BODY OF A GIRL P 459, $1.95

"Does what a good mystery should do: open up into all kinds of ramifications, with untold menace behind the action. At the end, there is a bang-up climax, and it is a pleasure to see how skilfully Gilbert wraps everything up." —*The New York Times Book Review*

Michael Gilbert (cont'd)

THE DANGER WITHIN   P 448, $1.95

"Michael Gilbert has nicely combined some elements of the straight detective story with plenty of action, suspense, and adventure, to produce a superior thriller."   —*Saturday Review*

FEAR TO TREAD   P 458, $1.95

"Merits serious consideration as a work of art."

—*The New York Times*

Joe Gores

HAMMETT   P 631, $2.84

"Joe Gores at his very best. Terse, powerful writing—with the master, Dashiell Hammett, as the protagonist in a novel I think he would have been proud to call his own."   —Robert Ludlum

C. W. Grafton

BEYOND A REASONABLE DOUBT   P 519, $1.95

"A very ingenious tale of murder . . . a brilliant and gripping narrative."
—Jacques Barzun and Wendell Hertig Taylor

THE RAT BEGAN TO GNAW THE ROPE   P 639, $2.84

"Fast, humorous story with flashes of brilliance."

—*The New Yorker*

Edward Grierson

THE SECOND MAN   P 528, $2.25

"One of the best trial-testimony books to have come along in quite a while."   —*The New Yorker*

Bruce Hamilton

TOO MUCH OF WATER   P 635, $2.84

"A superb sea mystery. . . . The prose is excellent."
—Jacques Barzun and Wendell Hertig Taylor, *A Catalogue of Crime*

Cyril Hare

DEATH IS NO SPORTSMAN   P 555, $2.40

"You will be thrilled because it succeeds in placing an ingenious story in a new and refreshing setting. . . . The identity of the murderer is really a surprise."   —*Daily Mirror*

DEATH WALKS THE WOODS P 556, $2.40

"Here is a fine formal detective story, with a technically brilliant solution demanding the attention of all connoisseurs of construction."

—Anthony Boucher, *The New York Times Book Review*

AN ENGLISH MURDER P 455, $2.50

"By a long shot, the best crime story I have read for a long time. Everything is traditional, but originality does not suffer. The setting is perfect. Full marks to Mr. Hare." —*Irish Press*

SUICIDE EXCEPTED P 636, $2.84

"Adroit in its manipulation . . . and distinguished by a plot-twister which I'll wager Christie wishes she'd thought of."

—*The New York Times*

TENANT FOR DEATH P 570, $2.84

"The way in which an air of probability is combined both with clear, terse narrative and with a good deal of subtle suburban atmosphere, proves the extreme skill of the writer." —*The Spectator*

TRAGEDY AT LAW P 522, $2.25

"An extremely urbane and well-written detective story."

—*The New York Times*

UNTIMELY DEATH P 514, $2.25

"The English detective story at its quiet best, meticulously underplayed, rich in perceivings of the droll human animal and ready at the last with a neat surprise which has been there all the while had we but wits to see it." —*New York Herald Tribune Book Review*

THE WIND BLOWS DEATH P 589, $2.84

"A plot compounded of musical knowledge, a Dickens allusion, and a subtle point in law is related with delightfully unobtrusive wit, warmth, and style." —*The New York Times*

WITH A BARE BODKIN P 523, $2.25

"One of the best detective stories published for a long time."

—*The Spectator*

Robert Harling

THE ENORMOUS SHADOW P 545, $2.50

"In some ways the best spy story of the modern period. . . . The writing is terse and vivid . . . the ending full of action . . . altogether first-rate."

—Jacques Barzun and Wendell Hertig Taylor, *A Catalogue of Crime*

Matthew Head

THE CABINDA AFFAIR   P 541, $2.25
"An absorbing whodunit and a distinguished novel of atmosphere."
> —Anthony Boucher, *The New York Times*

THE CONGO VENUS   P 597, $2.84
"Terrific. The dialogue is just plain wonderful."
> —*The Boston Globe*

MURDER AT THE FLEA CLUB   P 542, $2.50
"The true delight is in Head's style, its limpid ease combined with humor
and an awesome precision of phrase."   —*San Francisco Chronicle*

M. V. Heberden

ENGAGED TO MURDER   P 533, $2.25
"Smooth plotting."   —*The New York Times*

James Hilton

WAS IT MURDER?   P 501, $1.95
"The story is well planned and well written."
> —*The New York Times*

P. M. Hubbard

HIGH TIDE   P 571, $2.40
"A smooth elaboration of mounting horror and danger."
> —*Library Journal*

Elspeth Huxley

THE AFRICAN POISON MURDERS   P 540, $2.25
"Obscure venom, manical mutilations, deadly bush fire, thrilling climax
compose major opus.... Top-flight."
> —*Saturday Review of Literature*

MURDER ON SAFARI   P 587, $2.84
"Right now we'd call Mrs. Huxley a dangerous rival to Agatha Christie."
> —*Books*

Francis Iles

BEFORE THE FACT   P 517, $2.50

"Not many 'serious' novelists have produced character studies to compare with Iles's internally terrifying portrait of the murderer in *Before the Fact*, his masterpiece and a work truly deserving the appellation of unique and beyond price."   —Howard Haycraft

MALICE AFORETHOUGHT   P 532, $1.95

"It is a long time since I have read anything so good as *Malice Aforethought*, with its cynical humour, acute criminology, plausible detail and rapid movement. It makes you hug yourself with pleasure."

—H. C. Harwood, *Saturday Review*

Michael Innes

THE CASE OF THE JOURNEYING BOY   P 632, $3.12

"I could see no faults in it. There is no one to compare with him."
—*Illustrated London News*

DEATH BY WATER   P 574, $2.40

"The amount of ironic social criticism and deft characterization of scenes and people would serve another author for six books."

—Jacques Barzun and Wendell Hertig Taylor

HARE SITTING UP   P 590, $2.84

"There is hardly anyone (in mysteries or mainstream) more exquisitely literate, allusive and Jamesian—and hardly anyone with a firmer sense of melodramatic plot or a more vigorous gift of storytelling."

—Anthony Boucher, *The New York Times*

THE LONG FAREWELL   P 575, $2.40

"A model of the deft, classic detective story, told in the most wittily diverting prose."   —*The New York Times*

THE MAN FROM THE SEA   P 591, $2.84

"The pace is brisk, the adventures exciting and excitingly told, and above all he keeps to the very end the interesting ambiguity of the man from the sea."   —*New Statesman*

THE SECRET VANGUARD   P 584, $2.84

"Innes . . . has mastered the art of swift, exciting and well-organized narrative."   —*The New York Times*

THE WEIGHT OF THE EVIDENCE   P 633, $2.84

"First-class puzzle, deftly solved. University background interesting and amusing."   —*Saturday Review of Literature*

Mary Kelly

THE SPOILT KILL   P 565, $2.40

"Mary Kelly is a new Dorothy Sayers. . . . [An] exciting new novel."
—*Evening News*

Lange Lewis

THE BIRTHDAY MURDER   P 518, $1.95

"Almost perfect in its playlike purity and delightful prose."
—Jacques Barzun and Wendell Hertig Taylor

Allan MacKinnon

HOUSE OF DARKNESS   P 582, $2.84

"His best . . . a perfect compendium."
—Jacques Barzun & Wendell Hertig Taylor, *A Catalogue of Crime*

Arthur Maling

LUCKY DEVIL   P 482, $1.95

"The plot unravels at a fast clip, the writing is breezy and Maling's approach is as fresh as today's stockmarket quotes."
—*Louisville Courier Journal*

RIPOFF   P 483, $1.95

"A swiftly paced story of today's big business is larded with intrigue as a Ralph Nader-type investigates an insurance scandal and is soon on the run from a hired gun and his brother. . . . Engrossing and credible."
—*Booklist*

SCHROEDER'S GAME   P 484, $1.95

"As the title indicates, this Schroeder is up to something, and the unravelling of his game is a diverting and sufficiently blood-soaked entertainment."
—*The New Yorker*

Austin Ripley

MINUTE MYSTERIES   P 387, $2.50

More than one hundred of the world's shortest detective stories. Only one possible solution to each case!

Thomas Sterling

THE EVIL OF THE DAY   P 529, $2.50

"Prose as witty and subtle as it is sharp and clear. . .characters unconventionally conceived and richly bodied forth . . . . In short, a novel to be treasured."
—Anthony Boucher, *The New York Times*

If you enjoyed this book you'll want to know about
THE PERENNIAL LIBRARY MYSTERY SERIES

Buy them at your local bookstore or use this coupon for ordering:

Qty	P number	Price
———————	———————	———————
———————	———————	———————
———————	———————	———————
———————	———————	———————
———————	———————	———————
———————	———————	———————
———————	———————	———————
———————	———————	———————
———————	———————	———————
———————	———————	———————
———————	———————	———————
———————	———————	———————
———————	———————	———————
———————	———————	———————

	postage and handling charge	$1.00
	_____ book(s) @ $0.25	———————
	TOTAL	

Prices contained in this coupon are Harper & Row invoice prices only.
They are subject to change without notice, and in no way reflect the prices at
which these books may be sold by other suppliers.

**HARPER & ROW, Mail Order Dept. #PMS, 10 East 53rd St., New
York, N.Y. 10022.**
Please send me the books I have checked above. I am enclosing $_____
which includes a postage and handling charge of $1.00 for the first book and
25¢ for each additional book. Send check or money order. No cash or
C.O.D.s please

Name_____

Address_____

City_____ State_____ Zip_____
Please allow 4 weeks for delivery. USA only. This offer expires 4-30-84.
Please add applicable sales tax.